Special Delivery

Arnold J Miles

Published by Arnold J Miles, 2024.

This is a work of fiction. Similarities to real people, places, or events are entirely coincidental.

SPECIAL DELIVERY

First edition. June 24, 2024.

Copyright © 2024 Arnold J Miles.

ISBN: 979-8224383276

Written by Arnold J Miles.

Chapter One

My name is Tom.

Ever since the pandemic began, I have worked from home. I live alone in a small block of flats, and while it is a bit lonely from day to day it is generally fine. We can go into the office twice a week for "networking", but otherwise it is the usual principle: get out of bed and shower, walk to the living room, turn on the computer and prepare yourself for one more daily grind.

I hook up sometimes while I work from home, either with friends or through the apps. They're good fun and they break up the monotony sometimes. Otherwise, the only daytime interactions are virtual meetings or delivery drivers dropping off parcels either for me or for other people in the building who are not at home. Sometimes it can be two to three times a day that a friendly older delivery van driver rings my buzzer just to get into the building.

Today was one such day: I was in an online meeting when sure enough, the buzzer rang. It must have been about 25°c outside and even hotter indoors. I quickly jumped over to the buzzer to see who it was.

"Hey mate, I've got an Amazon parcel for flat three in your building but they ain't in. Could you take it?". He asked.

"Sure, come on up", I replied.

I opened the door and shouted down the stairs. "I'm just on a work call mate. The door's open!"

I put my headphones back on and got back to the work call when I saw the delivery man enter the door with a box.

And... oh no.

He was beautiful. He must have been at least six foot, white with a nice tan, naturally lean and fit but with a bit of additional gym muscle to go with it. He had short black hair, a strong jawline and a cheeky smile. He was wearing a white t-shirt that was sticking to him in the heat, with those workman's trousers that have pockets everywhere, and some comfy trainers. My cock twinged as he stood there.

He mouthed to me to ask if he could leave the parcel on the floor by the door. I nodded and smiled. He then tried to get my attention for something else. I made my excuses and momentarily left my online call.

"I'm really sorry mate, can I use your loo?" He asked. "I really need a piss".

"Of course!" I said, and pointed through to the bathroom, which was an en-suite straight past my bedroom.

I left him to it, fighting the urge to walk in the bathroom behind him.

A minute or so later, he returned. His face was wet and he had clearly splashed some cold water on his sweat-glistened face.

"Cheers mate," he said. "It's so shit sometimes being a delivery driver. You don't have a bathroom or all the usual stuff most workers have, and some people treat you like dirt".

"I totally understand," I replied. "Do you want a glass of water? It's roasting outside".

"Life saver mate, thanks".

I got him a glass and as I returned from the kitchen he was wiping his face with the bottom of his shirt. He revealed a hint of a six pack and a neat little downward trail of hair that made me fight the urge to fall to my knees. He pulled his shirt back down, gratefully drank the water and handed me back the glass.

"Thanks again mate, I really appreciate the help. I deliver in the area so I might well see you around again".

"Sure thing", I replied. "Drop in for a pitstop anytime you like".

I blushed at the cheesy piece of shitty twaddle that just left my mouth and instantly felt like a fucking idiot. He laughed, patted me on the shoulder and went on his way.

I quickly logged on to the apps on the off chance that the sexiest delivery guy I had ever seen was online, but alas he wasn't there.

Chapter Two

A few weeks went by. I thought occasionally about the friendly delivery guy, but he had not come back. It had been that hot a day when I saw him. Part of me wondered if I had invented him. Certainly, I felt like I had probably built him up to be a more attractive man than he actually was.

One late afternoon on a very quiet work day, I arranged a hook-up with a local friend. I had met him a few times and it was always good fun. Like me, he was in mid-twenties. He would come over and we would make out, sometimes I would suck him, sometimes he would suck me, and sometimes we would fuck. All quite unremarkable, but all pretty hot and reliable too.

This time, he was in a hurry and he just wanted to unload. I let him into my building and he came up to my flat. Literally as he closed the door, his belt was already undone and I could see his cock throbbing through his trousers. He kissed me while unzipping to reveal some rather fetching black briefs. His cock was around seven inches erect; a nice head with low hanging balls. It does the job nicely.

I got straight down onto my knees. As I unleashed his cock from his pants, he was already completely hard. I got straight to work. Just then the buzzer rang. I ignored it.

I loved giving head. There is just something about seeing a hard cock pointing right at you, knowing that you are the one giving instant pleasure to the man looking down at you, knowing that you are the one driving him crazy as your tongue caresses his balls, knowing that his cock will throb as it hits the back of your throat, knowing that you alone are responsible for him feeling relaxed later that night thanks to what you are doing to him in that very moment.

I knew that he was in a hurry, so I quickly thrusted back and forth. He fucked my mouth and our movements nicely aligned. His moans intensified as his precum leaked down my throat. Soon afterwards, he shot a warm load straight down my throat, holding the back of my head so I could take every last drop.

He withdrew his cock, playfully tossed his hands through my brown hair and zipped himself back up.

"Thanks mate, that was hot," he said. "See you again soon".

He kissed my cheek and left my flat. He must have been there all of five minutes. I love encounters like that. And who does it hurt? Nobody.

Later that evening I went out to meet a mate. As I left my building, I checked the outside postbox for my flat. There was a "Sorry we missed you" card from a delivery courier, which presumably got left after my buzzer had gone earlier. At the end of the card was a handwritten message.

"So much for a pitstop! Ha, sorry I missed you buddy"

Fuck. Off I went to meet my mates, my cock dripping as I wondered what might have been.

Chapter Three

A few more weeks passed by, and for much of it I was unwell with COVID. A bit of a weird feeling: not exactly like a cold, but not exactly like a flu either. Some days, I felt on the mend and that I was definitely improving, and then another day or so would pass and I would be struggling to stand up without feeling shaky and dizzy.

In the end, I was probably housebound with zero energy for about ten days. I watched TV, slept, watched TV again, then slept again. It was all a bit of a daze. I would check the apps - just for old times sake as much as anything - but I had no horn whatsoever. No longing for cock; just for sleep.

One of those miserable mornings, I was feeling particularly shit. The rain was pouring down outside along with occasional rumblings of thunder. My buzzer rang...

"Hey mate!" It was him. "It's been a while. I've got a delivery for the flat next door to you. Mind if I come in from the rain and leave it with you?"

I smiled for the first time in ages at hearing his voice.

"You can mate", I replied, "but I've got COVID and I'm feeling pretty rough to be honest. Can I let you in the building and you can just leave it by my front door? Sorry if you need the bathroom or a towel".

Up he came, and I heard the parcel gently drop to the floor. Then a tap on my flat door. I put a face mask on and opened it. There was a parcel and a few yards down the corridor was him: gorgeous, tall and athletic him. Friendly, caring, yet nonchalantly strong him. Dripping with rain, his hair had previously been quite short and spiky, but this time it was drooping over his forehead while rainwater soaked his t-shirt onto his body. He was masked as well and safely far away from me.

"So sorry that you're feeling shit mate," he said. "Do you need me to get you anything?"

What a gentle giant. Just give me your strong arms and your cock, please. Of course, that's not what I actually said.

"That's so sweet of you mate but it's fine. I've got friends who are delivering stuff for me. But thank you."

"All good," he replied. "You actually treated me like a human being rather than a delivery driver so I'm happy to return the favour mate. Pity I can't come in as I wouldn't mind a cuppa! Maybe next time".

"Genuinely any other time mate. Sorry".

He waved and his forehead gave the impression that he was smiling at me behind his mask... and then he was gone, off for another day of deliveries in the rain. I went back inside, for the first time in days feeling a spring in my step and just a hint of a twinge in my pants.

God, the effect he has on me. For a week I have barely ever been erect enough to piss any further than my shoes, and yet here I am in my living room holding a neighbour's parcel and sporting a hard-on. I looked out of my window and saw him running back to his van to avoid the rain.

I grabbed my crotch at the mere thought of taking his wet t-shirt off, and smelling him. I felt the excitement of just imagining what was underneath those pants of his. Was he hairy, was he shaven or was he smooth? Was he cut or uncut? Was he rough or was he gentle? Would he enjoy a man's touch? A man's tongue? Or was he just a friendly lad with zero interest in a man like me?

Before I could even contemplate the answers, I felt a bit dizzy again and I decided that I would spend the rest of the morning on the sofa. Thinking of him.

Chapter Four

I was starting to feel better, and even managed to make it out with a few friends last night.

My city's gay scene is far from perfect, but it's alright. There are five bars, all of varying styles and all dotted around various parts of the city centre. One is a traditional pub, one is a small bar for chatting, one is a dancing bar for younger people, one is a music bar and the last one is the biggest one that's suitable for a bit of a general dance and party.

It was this last one to which we decided to go tonight. We enjoyed a nice meal first and then headed in the direction of the bar for a cocktail and a bit of dance.

As we got to the entrance, I heard somebody shout from across the street.

"Hey!"

Jogging towards me was him. Tall, beautiful him. Smiling, strong him. Gentle yet giant him. Him.

He shook my hand. I tried to smile in a fashion that signalled something less filthy than "please please please won't you shoot in my hole". His handshake was firm yet friendly.

"I just realised that I don't know your name", he said. "I'm Matt".

Matt. Matty. Matthew.

"Tom. Nice to meet you", I replied.

He was wearing a tight fitting blue t-shirt and slim black jeans. His hair - no pouring rain this time - was back to being short and styled.

"Are you feeling better then?" he asked.

"Yes, thankfully!" I replied. "I've got my energy back and I just feel human. Thanks again for offering to help me. It was really kind of you".

"Anytime," he said. "It's just nice to see you on your feet. And nice to see you outside of a flat!"

We were interrupted by some other guys, who I guessed were with him. One called out:

"Oi Matt, are you coming to the pub or are you just gonna stand outside this puff house?"

I scowled at him.

"Don't talk like that please", I asked.

"I'm just having a laugh mate", he replied.

I was about to lecture him on the definition of laughter, but Matt got in before me.

"Dan, you're better than that. Apologise to him and his mates now."

"Matt, I was just..."

"Do it! These guys put up with more shit in five minutes than you'll ever have to in your life. Apologise."

"Okay, sorry. Guys, I'm sorry. I was just joking around but clearly it wasn't funny". He signalled to Matt and said, "look, just catch us up okay?"

Matt looked relieved as his mates wandered off. He took out his wallet and gave us some money.

"Tom, guys I'm so sorry. I'll have a word with him. He's harmless and he just doesn't think about these things. Not that that makes it any better, so please, just have a round on me".

"Matt, you don't have to do that. We don't need your money".

"I know", he replied. "A round of drinks is a piss poor apology. But please: take it".

He reached out to shake my hand. I accepted the invitation. My friends waved and wandered into the bar.

"Plus, I don't want to lose my pitstop, do I?" Matt grinned as he spoke to me.

We laughed and I felt confident enough to give him a hug. He wrapped around me with his arms. His cologne was strong, but not offensively so. He would turn a lot of heads that night beyond just mine.

He smiled and walked away, hopefully to lecture his mate Dan for the rest of the night on the still existing struggles of the modern homosexual.

Me and my mates went in and had a bit of a boogie, enjoyed the free drinks while my mates asked me who the sexy ally was, and eventually we went our separate ways home. As I got into bed, I smiled as my head hit the pillow.

Matt knew I was gay and he didn't care. Not only that, he respected me for it. He had every chance tonight to laugh nervously with his mate and walk away. He could have even frowned at him but said nothing, and I might not have called him out. He could have apologised to me without actually trying to correct the situation. But instead he stood up in front of his mates and put them in their place to defend some random bloke that once let him have a piss in his flat.

My cock still twitched at the whiff of his cologne and his arms around mine. But fuck, it felt good knowing that my cock was twitching at a decent bloke as well as a hot one.

Chapter Five

What is it that I feel for Matt?

Given the amount that I had drank, I woke up the morning after my night out feeling pretty fresh. I started to ponder my feelings for this guy in the cold and sober light of day.

It isn't love. I've been in love before. That's a story for another time.

No. It isn't love. I barely know him. I can live and breathe without him dominating my every waking minute. I freely and happily forget about him, then a little thing reminds me of him: a parcel, a glass of water, a random fit lad in the street. But Matt hasn't taken over my life.

No. It isn't love.

It's hard to call it a friendship either. Until last night, I didn't even know his name. He didn't know mine. He's just a nice guy who it turns out isn't a homophobic shit.

I mean, that's great, but no. I wouldn't yet call this a friendship.

Is it lust? Maybe. I do feel so excited by him. His body: naturally fit with just that hint of additional work from the gym. He's also inevitably strong from lifting parcels and boxes all day. His legs go on for days. His arms envelop you like one of his big delivery boxes. And his smile! Cheeky enough to lure you in, yet sincere enough to keep you looking. And looking. And looking.

And the straight factor has a certain appeal...

I'm merely assuming that he's straight, of course. I'm assuming he drinks and flirts with girls. I'm assuming he works out while checking out the tight arses of the girls at the yoga class happening next door to the weights room. I'm assuming he has women begging for a pounding and that on occasion he's only too happy to oblige.

It certainly does sound like lust, does it not...

Am I just as bad as his homophobic mate by assuming he's a pussy pounding lad? He could be anybody.

Yet there's something else about my feelings towards him. It's not necessarily anything remarkable. I just... like him. I see him and I feel lighter. He has a warming quality about him. I didn't doubt that he would defend me last night. I wasn't surprised when he asked if I needed any help or support recently when I was unwell.

Does he think about me in this way? Does he pick up his parcels each day hoping that I might be around to provide a cheerful pitstop on his journey? Did he hope that I was gay when he saw me last night? Does he care now that he knows that I am? Does he want my mouth, my arse, my cock? Or is he just... a guy?

My hookup app suddenly buzzed on my phone. It was a regular fuck buddy:

"Hey Tom, how's it going? You wanna come over?"

Right now? No. Sorry. Not for you.

I want to see Matt. I want to see him smile at me. I want to ask him about girls and guys and straights and gays and bis.

Maybe I am hopelessly in love. Maybe I just need to get on my knees in the back of his van and beg for a delivery just to get it out of my system. Maybe I just need to talk to him.

"Sorry mate, I'm a bit busy today. Have fun"

Chapter Six

The weekend came around again and I was having a lazy Saturday morning.

Some Saturday mornings I go for a run. Others I go to the gym. Others I wake up with the morning horn and try to do something about it. This morning? I had my feet up on the sofa reading a newspaper with a coffee. Old school, I know.

On weekdays, I shower the moment I awake but on Saturdays and Sundays I like to have a chilled morning and some breakfast first.

I sleep in my underwear, and this morning it was warm enough to wear just those and a thin white t-shirt while I read the paper. My underwear is almost exclusively tight-fitting trunks. I like how they feel.

I'm not super toned. Slim, more than athletic. Thin more than fit. But I'm in good shape. Guys that like to give sexual pleasure rather than receive it enjoy exploring my body. I'm tall, with strong legs and a reasonably grabbable arse. I have hair - dark brown - but not much of it, and I keep things pretty trimmed and tidy where it matters.

I was enjoying a sip of some juicy strong Colombian grind when the door knocked. Nobody ever knocked on my door directly. They always needed to ring the buzzer to the main building downstairs. It was a nice knock: loud enough to get my attention but gentle enough that had I been having a lie-in, I'd have barely noticed. Good knocker, whoever you are.

Without thinking much of it, I opened the door.

"Tom, I'm so sorry to disturb you... oh... hi".

It was Matt, and it was at this moment that we both realised that as we looked at each other from just a few feet apart that I was naked from the thighs down. I thanked the gay gods that I hadn't been thinking about him. He would have witnessed a flag pole.

"Oh my god. Sorry," I replied. "I shouldn't have answered the door like this. You could have been anybody".

I had just assumed that it would be a neighbour. Not that that would have made my appearance respectable. Although I reckon sexagenarian Mrs Barnstable downstairs would enjoy rolling back the years and grabbing a good eyeful if she had seen me looking like this. Saucy bitch.

But no. *He* had seen me like this. I was dirty, with messy hair and probably in need of some strong mouthwash. Fuck's sake, Tom.

"No, it's fine!" Matt helpfully interrupted my internal ranting. "Sorry, I would have buzzed but the main door was open. I've got a delivery for Flat 1 but they're not in. It's quite a few boxes I have for them... I was hoping I could leave them here?"

"Sure, no problem," I replied. "Should I come down and give you a hand?"

"Lifesaver mate, thank you. Maybe put some pants on. You'll have somebody's eye out".

Matt glanced down at my crotch with that cheeky yet so fucking annoyingly perfect and sincerely innocent grin.

"Shush!" I objected. "Some men would go weak at the knees for this sight on a Saturday morning".

"I don't doubt it! If you wouldn't mind helping, I'd owe you one".

I propped the door open - not with my massive cock before you get too filthy -, put some proper clothes on and went down to help. He was parked right outside, and sure enough there were half a dozen boxes waiting that could only be carried in one at a time.

Matt wore a cap to protect his head from the strong early morning sunshine, a tight fitting red t-shirt that hugged him like a mother terrified of losing their child, and jeans that begged the eyes to follow ever further up the thigh.

"More respectable?" I asked, pointing at my jeans.

"Yeah, I would be seen in public with you now", Matt quipped.

"Lucky you to have seen me in private", I quipped back.

Look at me. Flirting with the sexiest guy in town.

He smiled and handed me a box. Up and down the stairs we went. On the final trip, he locked the van behind him as he led us up to my flat. Did he want me to invite him in?

"Nice. Done. They're heavy! Thanks Tom".

"Anytime", I replied. "Do you want a cup of coffee?"

"Mate, I would love one but I need to get the rest of these deliveries done quickly. I'm babysitting my niece later".

My heart melted. Uncle Matt. God, I'm weak.

"I am glad I caught you though," said Matt. "I want to apologise again for the other night. It horrifies me that somebody I know would cause trouble for you and your friends".

"You really don't need to apologise".

"I think I do".

"Please, stop. My friends appreciated that you stepped in so quickly, not just to shut it down but to stop it happening again. They also spent all night asking how I knew you, and whether it was through filthy ways. They're a bunch of horny bastards, not the arbiters of moral decency".

"And what did you tell them?" Matt asked.

"I merely told them that you once had a piss in my vicinity and that they could decide for themselves whether that was innocent or kinky".

"Oh jesus! Speaking of which..." Matt looked towards the bathroom. "May I?"

I nodded and he went through to the bathroom. He really does seem sweet. He is a lad's lad, in that he's gym fit, he drives a van and he could probably crush me like a pea. But he is gentle and kind too. Which lucky person had or would get their way with him?

"Thanks Tom," Matt said as he returned to my living room. "I would genuinely like that coffee with you sometime. It is nice to talk with you. Let me give you my number".

He left his business card on the table. He went in to shake my hand just as I went to hug him. The result was an awkward brush of my crotch by his right hand.

"I think you're becoming a bit too obsessed with my crotch," I said.

"Oh fucking hell," he exasperatingly cried out while blushing. "I'm gonna go before I cause more chaos! Coffee sometime Tom, yeah?"

"Please," I replied. "Enjoy spending time with your niece."

He shut the door with a friendly wave. Off again came my jeans, and I lazily grabbed my semi through my underwear with one hand, while picking up his business card with the other.

"Matt Wilson - Deliveries and Removals"

I smelled the card hoping to get his scent, but all I got was paper.

He is beautifully innocent, yet relaxed too. And he would enjoy a coffee with me.

If it is merely lust that I'm feeling, it's the strangest lust I've ever known.

Chapter Seven

I decided to leave it a day before sending Matt a message late on a pleasant Sunday morning.

"Hey Matt, it's Tom," I wrote. "I won't push you on a coffee in case you were just being polite! But if you're still up for it I'd like that. I'll even put on some trousers..."

I sent the message, and decided to get on with my day. I was up and about, and I had already finished a good cardio session at the gym. The one I went to was part of a hotel complex. It wasn't the best gym in the world, but because it was part of a hotel it also had a swimming pool, sauna and steam room.

After a long stint on the rowing machine, I grabbed a quick shower, changed and then made my way to the sauna in my swimming shorts.

Truth be told, as much as I enjoyed thinking about Matt, by the time I wearily sat down on the hot wooden sauna benches I wasn't thinking about him or anything else at all.

I love sitting in this sauna. If it's empty, it's a nice space to switch off. If it's not, the people - mostly men - that usually come in here are quite cute: straight guys staying in the hotel as part of a stag weekend, discussing football, sex and lads lads lads; or cute couples who flirt with each other and have the occasional "secret" grope when they think nobody's watching.

Today, it was empty. To be fair, it was a warm summer Sunday and plenty of people would be out enjoying the weather. Just as I was sitting back and shutting my eyes, I heard the door open.

A man walked in, wearing tight shorts. They were one of those pairs that while they were technically black, they were accompanied by about fifty different bright colours all making pretty lines and patterns. He was probably in his thirties, with vibrant but well maintained ginger curly hair, a bare chest but with a hot trail of hair running down before being hidden by his shorts. He had a little bit of weight, but carried it wonderfully well. He clearly stayed fit; he was just beginning to see the effects of drinking and eating as well.

I had never seen him before, and couldn't help but enjoy the view from the corner of my eye.

"Hey, room for one more"? He asked. He sounded like he was from London, although he also had a soft and well-spoken tone.

"Good morning - of course!"

He sat on the bench directly opposite me, legs quite widely spread and with an air of confidence and comfort with his appearance. Given that he had greeted me as he walked in, I thought I would strike up a conversation.

"Are you a regular or staying at the hotel?" I asked.

"I'm staying here for a few days with work. Now COVID is hopefully fucked off, I travel around the country delivering training."

"That's cool. Although I expect that means lots of lonely time in hotels?"

"Sometimes it's a slog for sure. I miss my wife and kids."

"I bet. Sorry man".

"All good. How about you, are you local?"

"Yes, and very much not married".

"Not found the right girl?" He asked.

"Not found the right guy". I corrected him.

"Ah."

I was in a playful mood.

"All the finest ginger men are married with children already, you see".

He didn't react, except to rub some sweat off his chest.

"Is that right? Well, fair enough."

"I'm Tom", extending my hand to him.

He shook it without saying his name in return. How beautifully discreet.

"Nice to meet you, Tom. I should get going".

He quickly got up and strolled out. I was a bit taken aback, but nevermind. I had been a bit too forward. I shut my eyes for a few moments more then picked myself up off the sweat-filled bench and made my way back to the showers.

The changing rooms were starting to fill up now as the lazy Sunday gym goers were waking up from their morning hangovers and heading for a workout.

I passed the first few busy shower cubicles to find an empty one. They all had frosted glass doors and partitions, with a mirror at the end for the Instagram-selfie-towel-around-the-waist crowd.

As I walked towards a free cubicle, I passed a running shower with an open door. The unnamed man was facing the wall, with his arse in full view of anybody that walked past. And a truly beautiful arse too. The sort of arse you would gladly follow around a shopping centre no matter where it took you.

He turned only his head around, smiling at me with the knowing arrogance of a straight man who could call upon the services of any hungry gay he encountered in a city spa hotel. His curly hair was now wet and falling over his forehead.

"You took your time," he said.

"I... what?" I replied.

He turned his whole body around now, showing an erection that could have kept my propped door open for any box delivery yesterday. His dick was uncut, at least seven inches long, chunky too, with a beautiful little glistening tip thanks to the precum that had started to mix with the water. He kept his cock hair gorgeously trimmed. Quite thick right above his cock but completely shaven all around it.

He made no beckoning motion but I was drawn in like a moth to a curly, bright and flickering ginger flame. I walked in, closing the frosted glass behind me. I lobbed my towel over the door. I opened my mouth to remark that this was a pleasant turn up for the books, but he put his finger on my lips.

At this point, I should say that we all know what happens next.

I certainly know what happens next.

This is not my first time meeting a visiting stranger in these cubicles.

I was very, very ready to get on my knees, take his juicy cock in my mouth, swallow his load and then let him walk away, get dressed and phone his wife to say how much he missed her.

But this was not what happened.

He turned around, bent over slightly and spread his gorgeous, gorgeous arse. I think he must get it waxed, crack and all.

"Tongue my hole", he whispered into my ear.

I did not need persuading. I got on my knees, feeling the water trickle down to my face from the shower above. I stroked his calves with my hands. He washed his body with hot water as I enjoyed exploring him.

I continued to move my hands up his legs, settling for a nice while on his thighs. They weren't tree trunks, but they weren't breadsticks either. Just beautifully formed, lived-in chunky legs that it would have been a pleasure to massage. But that was not why I was there.

My eyes focused on my prize: a hole with just a hint of a pink tinge. A ginger stubble surrounded it that suggested he did indeed get waxed or shaved regularly. The lucky therapist who did that must have a few stories to tell.

I placed my tongue on his lower back, enjoying smelling that gym whiff combined with his freshly washed body. I worked my tongue down to his left cheek, giving it a playful little nibble. I did the same to the right cheek.

My left hand was under his balls, gently massaging his perineum with my thumb. His moans were getting more audible, and he quite clearly couldn't give a fuck about any fellow gym-goers that were occupying other shower cubicles.

I was so horny for him and I didn't need to spend hours hurting my knees on a hard shower floor. I got my tongue straight and deep into his hole. He jolted forward and put his hands on the shower wall. I got both my hands and spread his arse wide and spat on his hole. Another time, I would love to spread him on a hotel bed: rim him, finger him then fuck him. But for now, my tongue was the lucky part of my body doing the work. I stuck it as far into his hole as the angles would allow, vigorously moving it back and forth in and out of him.

For a second, I kneeled back just to enjoy the sight in front of me. But his moans almost became a demanding groan at the absence of my tongue on his hole.

"I'm gonna cum," he moaned quietly.

He quickly spun around. He had barely touched his cock but he was throbbing. Clearly this man enjoys the touch of a tongue.

Before I could stay there any longer just admiring his body, he thrust his cock into my mouth, grabbed the back of my head with his left hand and facefucked me. I saw his eyes were shut and he clearly didn't give one little bit of shit about me. I loved it.

Within just a few seconds, I was tasting his sweet load drenching my throat. I grabbed his arse cheeks as he shot, holding his cock in my mouth to enjoy every last drop. He was impressively silent as he came, only showing his release through his jolting movements and hot sweaty spunk. His arse clenched hard in my hands.

He almost fell over me as his hands grabbed my shoulders for support. He gently pushed my face off his cock, brought me to my feet and opened the door. He then turned around and continued his shower. The obnoxious fucking Adonis had got what he needed from me and I was worthless to him now. I both resented him and admired him. I would see him again in a heartbeat if he demanded it.

I jumped in the next door cubicle and took off my trunks with some difficulty. Tempting as it was to wank a load out right there and then, I decided to wait. I enjoy it much more to build up a load. That growing frustration I feel at not shooting a load is outweighed only by the satisfaction of knowing how violent the cum explosion is going to be for the lucky mouth or hole that eventually receives it.

Instead, I showered and tried to let my erection subside before returning to the changing rooms, where the married muscular ginge had already left. A couple of people looked at me, perhaps wondering if I was the cause of some of the audible shenanigans in the showers a few minutes earlier. I looked back with pride, trying to suggest with my eyes that any of them would be welcome to join me another time.

I got dressed, left and wandered home in the Sunday sun. My phone vibrated.

"Tom! Mate, I'd genuinely like that. You seem such a sound lad. How about next weekend?"

As much as I had just enjoyed my Sunday brunch from the obnoxious straight man, my heart jumped at the prospect of seeing another straight man - this one genuinely gorgeous and kind - in just a few days.

"Great! It's a date".

Chapter Eight

My week dragged on a bit at work, but all was generally fine. I went into the office for a couple of days and worked at home the rest. With the end of the week approaching, I started to think about Matt and my meeting with him.

Though I would love to spend the afternoon flirting with him and casually taking him back to my flat so I could be his first manhole, I absolutely did not expect that to happen. For so many reasons.

For one, he has given no sign of being attracted to me.

For another, if he might have been attracted to me, who's to say that I would be his first?

No. This man has literally had a drink of water in my flat and a piss in my toilet. Just because I want to have him sit on my face does not mean that he is thinking the same thing.

And yet... straight men would not usually want to go for a coffee with me alone. Straight guys might join me amongst a group of friends, sure. They might grab a drink with me if they already know me. But not a one to one introductory coffee.

As I enjoyed getting myself into such a tangle over nothing, my phone buzzed from a message.

"Hey mate, how's it going? It's Matt," it read. "Are you still up for a coffee this weekend? I'm free on Saturday afternoon if you are".

I text him back to confirm a time and to suggest a cafe for us to meet. I asked him how his week was going.

"Yeah, good mate!" He replied. "Although you have some competition for pit stops!". The text showed a laughing emoji. "I delivered a parcel today to this woman not far from you. She was probably about our age. She opened the door wearing a dressing gown, a bra and I assume some panties underneath! Gorgeous woman, blonde, slim etc. She's instantly flirting with me, even drops the pen to sign for the parcel and bends over slowly to pick it up!"

"Jesus!" I replied. "I hope you accidentally grabbed her crotch as a thank you?"

Another laughter emoji came back from Matt, followed by: "I think she was begging for it. Asked if I needed to run or did I want to stay and keep her company for a bit! She tried to stroke my arm."

"Well?! Did you?!" I asked urgently.

My cock was instantly hard at the idea of him dropping a load into some lucky girl.

"No! What do you take me for?" He replied.

"A horny stud who would have enjoyed himself?" I suggested.

"Haha, well thanks," he replied. "But no, not my style. I just collected the signature, wished her all the best and got the fuck out of there".

Oh my word. The deflation! Does this mean maybe I *would* be more his style? Or is nobody his style? Maybe he is just a nice, mild mannered guy?

"Well fair play mate," I eventually texted back. "Plenty of blokes in your situation would have jumped at the chance. Heck even this homosexual might have had a dabble!"

One more laughing emoji began his reply, followed by "I'll introduce you! No, it's not that sort of easy natural thing for me. To be discussed haha".

To be discussed? Oh lord.

I just wanna lap him up.

Chapter Nine

It was the night before my coffee with Matt. I had every expectation that this would be a simple, friendly and nice coffee. No footsie under the table, no "check please" and back to mine. Just a nice and pleasant coffee was all I expected.

As such, I really, really, *really* did not want to embarrass myself by being stupidly horny. I hadn't shot a load since before I had rimmed the married ginger sauna man. If I turned up horny, I would be at risk of being stupidly flirtatious and that did not need to happen.

I logged onto the apps, in search of what we shall call a strategic shag. I checked my favourites and sure enough, the friend who I sucked off last week was online.

"Hey, how's it going?" I asked.

"Good thanks man, you okay?" he replied.

"Yeah alright thanks. I could really do with you dumping a load in me. Wanna pop over?" I asked.

"Sure! On my way". He replied. Boom.

His name is Anthony. He's one of those guys that is a friend with benefits, with the emphasis heavily on the benefits. We don't really chat outside of the apps, although we follow each other on some socials and we like each other's stories, and if we see each other on a night out we'll have a friendly hug.

Nobody in our lives knows about what we get up to. We don't hide it, but we don't flaunt it either. It's a very functional friendship. You scratch my back, and I'll shoot a load over yours.

He rang my bell and I buzzed him into the building.

"I was hoping to see you online, Tom!" Anthony said. "How come you're so riled up tonight?"

"It's been a little while since I shot a load and you know I love your cock." I said in reply.

He pleasurably groaned with a smile on his face and came with me to my bedroom. We kissed passionately as he pulled my jeans off to reveal some nice black trunks. He flipped me over and pushed me onto the bed.

Anthony really did love my arse. He started at my calves and worked his way up, kissing and licking every part of my legs. His hands wandered around my inner thigh, which always got me so riled up.

He massaged my arse over my underwear. He is such a teasing man. Some playful slaps of my arse left me begging him to take my pants off. He duly obliged, and I could feel the warm breath of his moaning as he placed his mouth over my hole. He slapped me again and he knew that for the next few moments I was merely putty in his hands.

His head retreated a fraction as he surveyed my arse and legs in all their glory. My body will never make the front page of Attitude, but if you're somebody who likes strong thighs and a nice round arse with a little bit of hair on them, I'm your kind of guy. He slapped my cheeks again and finally - thankfully - he couldn't resist the urge much longer: his tongue fell deep into my hole and I moaned loudly into my pillow.

"Oh fuck, Anthony," I cried. "God I love it when you do that".

We really did have a nice chemistry. I doubt we had ever had a meet that ever lasted more than half an hour, but we regularly met each other's needs and he was meeting mine wonderfully right now.

Anthony stood up and took his clothes off. I was about to turn over to get on my knees, but not this time.

"Don't move," he gently commanded me.

I closed my eyes, and a moment later his lubed finger was making its way deep into my hole. I was in heaven. He pounded me with his forefinger.

I love being rimmed and fingered. I still remember the first time a guy did it to me. I was terrified, and he didn't even fuck me. Now, if a guy wanted to play with my arse all night I would let him, no matter who it was. Heck, I might even let that horny woman who tried to get Matt out of his delivery clothes the other day play with my arse if she was good with her tongue.

A bit more lube, and Anthony nibbled gently on my ear.

"You ready?" He whispered.

I weakly nodded into my pillow. He slowly eased his cock in.

"Oh my god, yes," I breathed. "Please fuck me".

Wow. I turn into a right needy bitch when I'm turned on. Quickly, Anthony was inside of me, fucking me powerfully and deeply. I can take a cock pretty well these days and his seven inch cock was the perfect size for me: more than big enough to feel it, but not big enough to cause a problem.

He gave his arms a rest and lay down right on top of me. He pulled my arms above my head and held on to my hands while his cock thrusted in and out of me. I could feel his sweat drip down my back. His grunts felt so hot on my neck.

He moved back up on to his knees and fucked me at a forty five degree angle, slapping my arse a few more times while doing so. He was playfully dominant with me in a way that friends with benefits could be: it was effortlessly comfortable, relaxed and horny.

"Turn over," he said.

He flipped me around, put a touch more lube on his cock and then he was straight back in. I moaned loudly - I found cock in missionary a little bit more challenging - but he (rightly) took this as permission to fuck me harder. He had his eyes closed as he pounded my hole.

I wondered: of whom he was thinking? Who was his Matt?

I was rock hard myself at this point and my cock flailed around as he fucked me. My pre-cum leaked out all over my stomach with every thrust.

"Wow, that's a lot of precum," Anthony observed.

He momentarily stopped, lapped it up with his fingers and then drenched my tongue with my own precum. He lent in and kissed me.

"Tom, this feels amazing," he said.

I was breathing heavily and almost finding it difficult to reply. "I'm struggling to hold my load in much longer," I eventually managed to say.

That was enough to make Anthony groan and want to shoot. I generally like to see someone else come first. I like to see their faces. I want to see that mix of agony and ecstasy that is never replicated in any other action, and use that to spur me on.

But as Anthony pounded me harder and harder, still with his eyes shut I too shut mine and Matt suddenly appeared in my mind. It was Matt that was pounding me now, thrusting and looking deep into my eyes. I could see him, smell him, feel him. He cheekily smiled at me as he fucked me, knowing that we were locked as one and that I was entirely his.

Thinking about Matt in that way took me over the edge and I was now uncontrollably shaking as I involuntarily shot my load all over me. Spurt after spurt flew out, some reaching my neck, most landing everywhere in the vicinity.

My arse clenched as I came, which was enough to take Anthony over the edge with me. I opened my eyes to see his face redden and he was about to shoot.

He shot a hot load right up my arse, almost falling over me as he did so. He mustered the energy to kiss me on the cheek, then licked up as much cum as he could find. Greedy slut.

He gently eased his dick out.

"Wow," I sighed. "Fuck, that was nice."

"It was," he breathlessly replied. "Thanks for having me round."

"Anytime mate." I smiled and kissed him again.

From here, we followed the same routine that we had done a few times before. We jumped in the shower together and washed each other clean of our filthy fluids. Anthony occasionally even had his own towel, if he was around that often. Sometimes, it was two or three times a week if we were in the mood.

He dried off and started to put his clothes on.

"You never shoot a load like that. You really are fucking horny tonight aren't you?" He asked.

"Ha - I guess so," I replied. "I just felt it".

I did indeed feel something, and it was indescribable. Anthony left and I went to bed, thinking about how much Matt jolted me and turned me on. And yet, I was genuinely just looking forward to coffee with him tomorrow and hearing his stories.

I fell asleep within seconds of my head hitting the pillow.

Chapter Ten

The day arrived. Some actual planned and wanted time with Matt, rather than a series of chance visits and encounters. I woke up feeling well rested and refreshed. I usually woke up feeling good after a nice fuck, and last night had been really nice.

I had my morning coffee, caught up on the news, and chatted to some friends. It was a nice lazy weekend morning.

I stayed casual. A plain white t-shirt, some tight blue jeans and trainers. Regular trunk underwear. No jocks, no revealing vests, no short shorts. Casual. Calm. Relaxed. At least in appearance...

I got there a few minutes early - us gays need to keep up our punctual reputations - but Matt was already there. Keen.

He had gone for the same casual look - t-shirt, jeans and trainers - but he pulled it off so much better than me. He wasn't insanely fit, like those guys that almost spend too much time on their body. No, he just gave you enough hints that underneath his clothes was a hot body of a hot guy. Maybe he was wearing a jock, I wondered as my eyes drifted down his body.

"Hey!" he smiled as he called towards me.

He saw me, stood up and initiated a warm hug. He really did just wrap around me in a snug fit that made you feel safe. And horny. Safely horny.

"Hey Matt, nice to see you. How's your day going?" I asked.

"Really nice. I was delivering this morning."

"Oh yes? Did you stumble across anymore half-naked horny girls?"

He laughed. "Thankfully not. It was *so* awkward. She looked offended, like she's not used to guys saying no. I think she thought that I was some arrogant lad who thought he was too attractive for her."

"Maybe you were?" I proffered.

"No! It's just not my style," he replied.

"Maybe some other delivery guy was lucky! Now, what would you like to drink?" I asked.

"You don't need to do that".

"Yes, I do. Because then you owe me, and your pride will make you stay for another".

I got us some coffee and sat back down. We enjoyed quite idle chat for a few minutes about deliveries and weather. Matt had initially worked solely in the removals trade, first with his Dad and now on his own since his Dad retired. However, COVID had made that line of work temporarily untenable and ever since he has done door-to-door deliveries, with the occasional well-paid removal job alongside.

All nice and simple so far. I think we were both maybe looking for a route into something more personal and relevant.

Matt went for that sort of question first.

"Do you mind if I ask you questions about your personal life?"

"No, go for it. I'm open with people I respect and trust".

"Do you respect and trust me?"

"Of course I do".

"Ha. Suuuccckker". He said, playfully.

God, if you only knew.

He continued. "My mate was a dick to you the other day. Is that common? How often do you get shit like that?"

"Nowadays, not so often. I've friends who grew up in the seventies and eighties. They had it bad. They used to get beaten up occasionally if they dared to be open about their sexuality, and even if they were quiet about it, they would still get shouted at in the street".

"I don't get that nowadays much," I continued. "I get the occasional comment. Somebody in the street drunkenly threatened to punch me once for being a faggot, but I felt confident enough that he was all talk. When I challenged him, he quickly backed off and walked away".

"I'm so sorry you need to do that, Tom". He looked genuinely hurt.

"It's okay. I mean, it's not okay obviously, but I'm comfortable. I can live my life. I can hold hands with who I want, I can kiss who I want, I can fuck who I want, and I can flaunt around town with a rainbow flag. Life's fine".

Matt smiled. "Well here's to people flaunting and fucking who they like". He clinked my coffee cup as he took a drink. "And do you? Flaunt and fuck?" He asked.

"Yes," I replied. "Well, sometimes. I'm quite relaxed about sex and sexuality. I don't think it's some big ethical betrayal to find multiple people attractive and interesting. I don't know that I flaunt it much, though".

He smiled, nodding to suggest that he understood me.

"Do you mind that I'm like that?" I asked.

"No! God no. No judgement from me, and I'm interested to be honest."

"Thank you. Can I ask you a personal question in return?"

"Sure".

"Do you like to flaunt and fuck? I'm assuming that you're straight?"

Matt nodded.

"And yet," I continued, "You had a sexy woman offering herself to you this week, and you walked away?"

He took a deep breath, looking down at his mug. He looked quite pensive, almost as if he was struggling to answer. I quickly jumped in.

"You obviously don't need to answer that if you don't want to".

"No, it's okay. I just don't talk about this stuff much. For some reason, I trust and respect you too". He smiled that cheeky smile again.

"I've never really done the whole sleeping around thing," he continued. "It's not my style. All my mates do, well most of them try to anyway. I'm sure most of them aren't very good at it! All of them would have said yes to that woman whose door I knocked on yesterday, given half a chance. I've just always preferred getting to know somebody properly first and respecting those boundaries".

Matt paused to sip some more coffee, pondered for a while to see if I had any questions or if I just wanted to continue listening. Having realised I could listen to him indefinitely, he carried on.

"I fell in love quite early. I was nineteen. I was at a pub quiz with some mates and one of them brought a friend along."

He was instantly smiling in that way that suggested something deeper.

"She sat next to me and introduced herself with a gorgeous smile. Emma. I remembered she gently touched my arm as she said my name.

She was so beautiful. I just fell weak at the knees. You know that feeling: how am I sitting next to somebody so beautiful and why the fuck are they voluntarily sitting next to me?"

I smiled and nodded knowingly.

"We just had a wonderful time all night. We did shit in the quiz! I don't think my mates were too happy that I was distracting this woman who was the most intelligent one there and probably knew most of the answers. But we didn't really care. She gave me her number at the end of the night and it took all my effort not to message her as soon as she left".

"That sounds wonderful. It sounds like you met again?" I asked.

"Yeah. We clicked instantly and within a few weeks we had already gone on holiday together and it was just amazing mate".

"How old was she?" I asked.

"Twenty," he replied. "A few months later, we moved in. Before that, I was living at home with my parents working for my Dad's removals firm. He's mostly retired now and I sort of run the business. So yeah, my first time living with someone and it was her. And we never looked back really. Waking up next to her every morning was just wonderful mate. I know I sound soppy but it was just like a dream".

I smiled.

"I proposed to her the following summer. We went on holiday to a resort in Greece. The sun was setting and we were looking out over the sea. She said yes!"

"Of course she did".

"Ha. Thanks. We got married when I was twenty and she was twenty three".

He showed me a photo from their wedding day. They were a gorgeous couple.

"That's amazing. And young! How old are you now?"

"I'm twenty six".

Matt wasn't wearing a wedding ring, and I don't think that I had seen him wearing one at any point since I had first met him.

I did not know exactly how this story would end, but I knew it would not end happily.

"We were out one day and she very quickly just felt unwell. Awful headache, sickness, dizziness etc. We got home and she took some heavy painkillers and eventually she was okay, but it was something different to anything she had ever had before. A week later, the same again but this time worse. She couldn't see straight or look anywhere without feeling dizzy".

"I got her to a GP the next day and she was quite worried by how quickly symptoms were developing and she arranged a scan for her. Within a few days, she'd had a seizure and was rushed to hospital. A brain tumour".

"She died three months later".

I stayed silent and just looked at him. His expression was weary, like a man who had told this story too many times, played it through his mind too many times, lived it too many times.

"Matt, I'm so sorry. And I'm sorry for making light of the encounter with that woman yesterday".

He smiled.

"Hey, that's fine. I'm just sorry for bringing the mood down from fucking and flaunting! There's no easy way to tell it."

"When did she die?"

"Two years ago. Just before the pandemic started".

"And... I don't know what to ask. I have questions but... do you even want to discuss this with me?"

"Yes. And no. Then yes. Ha. It's hard". He was fighting the urge to cry, but managing successfully for now. "Can I be honest with you?"

"Of course," I replied.

"My mates were as good as they could be. We spent the pandemic playing video games online. I moved in with my brother, his wife and my niece, so I had company during lockdown. It was fine".

"But... none of them are that great when it comes to emotional stuff. My mates are pretty shit with it, my brother is a nice lad but a bit emotionally useless, and my sister-in-law was struggling with being a parent of a young kid during lockdown. And nevermind the fact that I'm shit at this too. So I've sort of just built up a lot of stuff that probably I'm still making sense of".

He continued: "You can obviously tell me to fuck off, but I got a sense that you're a good guy, and quite different to a lot of my friends".

"You mean, I'm a slutty queer?" I smiled.

"Ha. Oh jesus. No. I don't know how to explain it. Just... nice. And understanding. I just got a vibe from you that we clicked a bit and might get on".

"Thank you. I felt the same". I said.

"So I'm not here to just use you as a therapist or anything. If it feels like that, I'm sorry. We can end this now if you like".

"Of course not". I reached out and touched his arm. He momentarily held my hand with his, then I retreated my hand back to my coffee.

"But I just got a sense that we would get on," Matt said, "and occasionally I guess that if I maybe talk to you a bit more personally than I would with my mates, then I might feel a bit better. If that's okay".

I smiled, nodding.

"Alright. Good". He clapped his hands together to break a bit of an intense few minutes. "Another coffee?"

I smiled again, nodded again. He went to the bar, returning a few minutes later with two coffees and some cake.

"If I'm gonna burden you with dead wife stories, the least I can do is buy you cake".

"Thanks," I smiled. "Can I ask another personal question?"

Matt nodded. "So long as I can have some cake first".

"Go ahead!" I smiled. "You're clearly not ready to shag a woman who wants a quick thing when you deliver a parcel. But... what are you ready for? How do you feel about..."

I hated myself in advance for using the words, but Matt jumped in to say them for me. "Moving on"?

"Yeah," I replied. "How do you feel about feeling something for somebody else?"

"I don't know, honestly. Usually I'm just thinking about it in the hypothetical, guessing how I will feel in a moment that never actually happens. That woman this week, that was just never something I would want to do anyway."

He paused, then continued.

"I hope you don't think this too weird, but the first time I felt anything like this was meeting you. And I don't mean anything physical by that".

"You can mean anything physical you like with me, Matt".

He smiled.

"I felt a warmth from you, as if I would be more comfortable being around you. I've not really been vulnerable around anybody since Emma. Even with my brother, I've put on a brave face rather than open up."

"With you," he continued, "I just had a feeling that I didn't need to worry about where a conversation would go. Sorry, I'm talking shit here".

"You're really not," I replied. "I've wondered about what sort of guy you are. At times, I've probably unfairly given you the lad-about-town stereotype in my head, and then I've been surprised you've been so nice to me. I cannot imagine what you've gone through in the last couple of years. And I feel a warmth towards you too. I won't lie that the first time I met you, that was in a "fuck me, you're hot" kind of way".

He laughed, shyly.

"But more generally," I continued, "I've just found you to be somebody that I like thinking about and I feel happy seeing you. So if you do feel comfortable opening up around me, I will do whatever I can to help. I don't really know what that looks like in practice".

"Me neither", Matt replied. "It might just be hanging out and seeing where conversation takes us."

"I'd like that. I don't mean this jokingly, but I guess I don't mean it super seriously either... are you comfortable being vulnerable around me, a gay guy who happens to think that you're stunningly beautiful?"

"You think I'm stunningly beautiful?"

"Ha. I think you're a gorgeous, gorgeous man. I guess the difference between me and the delivery woman is that I am at least trying to respect the rest of you too".

He went a bit red, but with the very quiet confidence of a man who had been told things like this before.

"Thanks Tom. No, I don't care one bit about your sexuality, except that I respect it. Part of me maybe feels more comfortable, truth be told. I like that you felt you could touch my arm before. I like that it can just be relaxed without necessarily having to mean anything."

"I think this conversation is probably a fair indication that we're comfortable around each other". I suggested.

He smiled. From there, our conversation drifted through a few other pleasantries and details. We agreed that we would hang out again sometime soon.

We got up to say our goodbyes, and we had a warm embrace. Matt held the hug for longer than I might have expected. But then today, he had shown a greater warmth and commitment to each other than I might have ever expected.

"Thank you, Tom. I don't know why, but I feel like I've got a bit of a weight off my mind."

We went our separate ways, and I walked home reflecting on how I felt about him. When he had left my sight previously, I had had erections, I had felt lust, I had felt intrigue... and now, I just realised that I had met an extraordinarily resilient man who had decided to put some trust in me.

To think I had felt the need to have sex just to suppress my horn, when this guy had possibly spent last night wondering how to tell me about the love of his life and how he misses her.

And yet he wanted to. He felt something for me that he had not felt for other people in his life. Even for a heartless and individualistic sod like me, it was - nearly - enough to bring me to tears.

Chapter Eleven

I slept well, although a few thoughts had been swirling around my mind about Matt.

We had had very different lives for people who were about the same age. He grew up in the same city in which he now lived. He had possibly been earmarked for the family business, and to which he had put his life into building for his own family, then COVID messed up the business part, and cruel circumstance messed up the family part.

Meanwhile, I had grown up somewhere else, moved here for university and then stayed. He married his teenage sweetheart, while I slept around and enjoyed the liberties that came with that.

And yet, these differences played their part in our connection. He felt like he could open up and confide in me without me judging him or at least without much consequence for the rest of his personal life. And for me, I had time and respect for him. So much of his life is wonderful and yet constricted, and then he has had to deal with so much shit, yet he has still come through it with an outlook that is kind and warm.

I cannot lie to you and say that his sweet peachy arse and jawline aren't an added bonus...

My phone buzzed.

"Hey Tom. Thanks again for yesterday. I hope I didn't scare you off."

I texted him back quickly.

"Hey, who dis? I got you saved in my phone as "Fuck and Flaunt"."

A laughing emoji came back in reply. I followed up with words.

"You didn't scare me off at all. Honestly, I was a little tearful at how you felt about opening up to me."

"Oh mate, I cried quite a bit myself last night. I don't know exactly what I was crying about tbh".

"Probably just a weight off your mind?"

"Yeah I guess. These last two years, family and mates keep asking me how I am, how I'm holding up and I just don't have a good answer. They mean well but I think they're waiting for me to have some perfect explanation of grief and I don't have that. With you, I can just chat shit and it's nice".

"Well, thank you. What are you up to today?"

"I'm babysitting my niece. I still live with my brother's family. How about you?"

"That's cool that you do that for your brother. I might see a mate later or hookup with someone. If it bores you a bit me saying stuff like that, I don't need to discuss it".

"Don't worry mate - you don't need to hear about my niece watching shit on TV but I'm telling you! Will you meet somebody you know, or a stranger?"

"Depends - I usually don't meet anybody. Some people are flaky or we just have a nice chat. But maybe I'll meet someone. let's see."

"#fuckandflaunt", he replied.

My turn to send the laughing emoji.

"Would you fancy hanging out one night this week? We could just watch a film or something? I'd have to come to you, if that's okay".

"I'd like that mate. I'll cook or get some food in. Obviously, as a gay we have to either watch a shit rom com or gay porn."

"Hahahaha. I'm in your hands mate".

We agreed on a day and time.

"I just wanna say, Matt: I'm not expecting that every time you meet me that you open yourself up and we have a deep conversation. No pressure or stress from me".

"Thanks Tom. I'm genuinely just looking forward to a movie and chilling out. All good."

"Okay great. Looking forward to it x"

I slacked off from browsing the apps, and just had a nice feel of my cock while thinking about Matt. I've had worse mornings.

Chapter Twelve

It was a pretty ordinary day at work (from home) without much happening. Another delivery driver dropped a parcel off during the morning. He didn't excite me that much.

I would be hanging out with Matt this evening. I was quite relaxed. Maybe I should be nervous, but everything that had gone before told me that I had no need to be. I was already feeling pretty horny long before Matt arrived, which maybe wasn't the most sensible thing to have allowed to happen.

Matt rang my bell and came up to my flat at around seven thirty that evening. He took his trainers off and left them at the door. He had a striped t-shirt on with particularly short sleeves, jeans and some white ankle socks revealed now that his shoes were off.

"Hey!" Matt gave me a warm embrace as he came through my door. "I don't know what you drink, but I brought some beers".

"Thanks Matt! Beer is great with me".

Over dinner, we discussed our days and he was very kind about my quite basic provision of a meal. I had made some simple chicken on top of some new potatoes and greens. I didn't want to assume he had an extensive palate only for him to politely shuffle the food about his plate. Thankfully, the dish went down well.

We sat across from each other at my very small dining table. I went for conventional room lighting. No candlelight. No mood music. It was friendly and civilised. Matt talked to me about how he still lives with his brother, and his wife and child.

"They have been so great to me," he said. "When Emma was really ill and in hospital, they told me that I could stay with them for as long as I needed to. I think we all thought that might be just a few weeks and then I would head home and start to sort my shit out. Then COVID came and it was a lockdown, so I made a bit of a snap decision to rent out our flat to a colleague who had a vulnerable relative who needed somewhere to be able to self-isolate for a while, and I just stayed with my brother and his family. I wouldn't say it was ideal! But it was probably better than being on my own."

I nodded, knowing exactly what he meant. I could certainly relate to that. Living alone during the various iterations of lockdown had been a lonely and difficult experience.

"Did you think about living with someone else? Like family or friends?" Matt asked.

"I definitely thought about it," I replied. "But there just wasn't an obvious option for me. Other like-minded friends live in similarly nice but small one-bed flats like this one. And while I love my family, they live hundreds of miles away. Even doing everything virtually, I still like my home and I wasn't ready to give that up".

"Yeah. I can imagine it was lonely though".

"Yeah", I replied, "but it was difficult in different ways for everyone. Every bit of my life was alone. But I know friends who didn't get to be alone for one second. They didn't have a single moment when they weren't in somebody else's physical space. One mate of mine has three kids in a small house, the oldest of whom was four years old during lockdown. I know how much he absolutely adores his children, but even he was going crazy a few weeks in".

"You're very understanding to think about it like that". Matt suggested.

"I might be now," I smiled, "but at the time, I was probably a miserable shit. Endlessly bored. Endlessly horny. The government prioritised grandparents seeing their grandkids, but they didn't think about the needs of the horny people living alone".

Matt laughed. "That's very fair. And now we've got some freedoms back, you're fucking and flaunting?"

"Occasionally". I smiled as I replied.

We finished dinner and agreed to watch an action film that had recently gone on the various streaming platforms that Matt had wanted to see for a while. I was grateful for having a definite suggestion. I got us both a beer, and we sat on the sofa. I intentionally sat at the opposite side, and popped some popcorn on the middle seat between us.

The film was pretty good to be fair. A getaway driver is thrown into an unfortunate set of circumstances when a heist goes wrong and he is left as the guilty party. With a car full of cash and no idea who framed him, it's up to him to figure out what happened, even though he has no idea who to trust.

Within the first half an hour or so, we had finished the popcorn and I moved the bowl to the floor.

"Do you mind if I put my feet on the sofa?" Matt asked. He smiled and curled his feet up where the popcorn had been. I have always found feet to be quite an off-putting part of the human body, but I cannot deny that Matt was testing my aversion at that moment.

The film continued. The getaway driver had - unbeknownst to him - been tailed by a motorcyclist, who was now shooting at him. Thankfully, he managed to outmanoeuvre him and escape. He eventually drove to somebody that he suspected of double crossing him and forced him into his car at gunpoint.

"Cheery film, isn't it!" I quipped. Matt laughed.

I went to the bathroom, and came back via the fridge, getting us both another beer. Matt gratefully accepted the beer as I sat down.

He rearranged his position and his cushion so that he was now facing across the sofa from me. He smiled at me as he moved his feet to lie across my thighs, looking at me to check it was okay. I smiled and nodded.

I now had one hand on my beer and one hand on his calves. His calves were wonderfully tight. I knew Matt enjoyed going to the gym occasionally, and he obviously spent plenty of time deadlifting heavy boxes for work. The result was legs that really wouldn't be out of place on a footballer.

Do you even care about the film? If you do: the getaway driver has just found a tracking device in one of the bags of money, and decided to throw all the bags out of the car and set them on fire.

"Fuck! Fuck no. I would not have done that". Matt said.

His legs were now firmly nestled on top of mine, with both my arms resting on his calves. I moved one arm slightly above his knee so that it was resting at the bottom of his thigh. I wasn't purposefully looking to tease him. It was just more comfortable for my arm.

Matt's jeans had moved up a little as he had shuffled on the sofa, and combined with his ankle socks he was showing me a nice patch of calf to rub. I relaxedly and rhythmically moved one of my hands so that they massaged his left calf just a little. I glanced sideways to make sure Matt wasn't uncomfortable. He was enthralled in the film and clearly very comfortable. As was I.

The film had taken a dark turn. The gang leader has now been identified to us all, and quite understandably he would like his money. He had the getaway driver's daughter kidnapped. I carried on enjoying the film, while nonchalantly gently massaging Matt's legs. As the getaway driver got more and more panicked, Matt looked ever more comfortable.

"Enjoying yourself?" Matt asked as he looked over at my hands.

"Sorry!" I replied. "It's just a natural reaction. I'm not trying to 'woo' you".

Matt smiled as he replied. "It's alright. It feels quite nice actually".

"Don't say that," I said. "I'll be wanking you off by the end of the movie".

Matt laughed and finished his beer. "To be fair, the last half an hour has probably been the most intimate experience I've had in about three years".

It was a casual and throwaway line, but fucking hell. That cut me quite deeply.

Matt went to the fridge himself and brought us back the last two beers of the pack. He sat back down, resting his legs exactly where they had been, pointedly looking at me until I put my hands back exactly how they had been before he stood up. We both laughed. I liked how comfortable he felt around me.

The getaway driver discovered that rival gangs had been trying to deceive him and get the money. He had cleverly led them to each other, where one gang wiped out the other and his daughter escaped. The film ended with the driver and his daughter walking away hand in hand.

We both smiled at the happy ending.

"I enjoyed that," I said.

"Yeah me too." Matt replied.

He stretched his arms out and stifled a yawn.

"Fair play mate, I'm really fucking comfortable now" he laughed. "I could just fall asleep". He briefly curled over onto his front, giving me a closer view of his gorgeous arse than I had yet had the chance to enjoy.

"You can, if you like," I said. "You're welcome to stay over anytime".

He smiled at me.

"It is a comfy sofa, to be fair". He said.

"I've a big bed and I'm a heavy sleeper. You could just jump in with me. I won't force my cock in your mouth in the middle of the night; don't worry."

Matt laughed. "Keep stroking my legs like that mate and you'd not have to force me".

We both laughed. Matt eventually said. "Thank you, but I think I'll head home. Early start tomorrow".

He stood up and put his trainers on as he got to the front door.

"Tom, thank you. I had a great night."

He gave me a hug.

"You give great hugs, you know that?" I said, still in his arms.

He laughed, and as he pulled away I could see him grinning cheekily at me in a way that made my mouth smile, my heart melt and my arse twinge.

"You're easily pleased!" He replied. "Goodnight mate".

"Goodnight Matt".

He gave me his customary wave and I watched his lovely arse follow the rest of him down the stairs.

My cock was naturally semi-erect at the physical contact I had just shared with him. I sighed in agonising pleasure.

I logged onto the apps, seeing if anybody was nearby. Within about ten seconds, a new message came in from a guy who was less than two hundred metres away.

"Hey mate, you seem close," it read. "Do you want a blowjob? No lights, no faces. Dark room BJ. Walk in, unzip, give me your load and go".

Just what the doctor ordered.

I gave it a few minutes before leaving just to make sure Matt had actually gone far enough away not to spot me. Not that it necessarily mattered, but we didn't need that interaction. I got to the guy's front door within five minutes, my cock still semi hard from being with Matt and now from the excitement of what was to come as well.

The door was unlocked. I walked in, shut it behind me. It was dark but there was still a bit of light from the passage window. I heard a whisper from the door to the left in front of me.

"In here," he said.

I walked in. Ah. Now it was genuinely dark.

"Hey," I heard him whisper.

I undid my belt and my top jeans button, and pulled my zipper down. He did the rest, pulling my jeans down to my ankles. Keeping my pants on, he started to feel around my cock, sniffing my crotch as he did so.

I gently felt his head. He was bald: maybe an older guy. His head was very pleasantly smooth, like he took care of himself. I felt around towards his face and felt a hint of stubble. His hands felt my thighs and I could hear his heavy breathing as a signal of his horn.

He pulled my pants down and he moaned as my dick popped out. My cock is about seven inches long, uncut with regularly trimmed dark pubes. My balls hang quite nicely below my dick. I'm not the most hung guy in the world but everything is nicely proportioned.

"Fuck. Yes," he whispered as my cock gently hit his face.

His hands left me and there was a brief second where I couldn't feel anything on me or near me. As I got ever so slightly nervous about what he was going to do to me, I felt his mouth surround my cock and without hesitation he was deepthroating me right to the very base.

"Oh my god, that's nice." I gently gasped and grabbed his head and kept it at the base of my dick.

He slowly pulled his head back and then quickly rammed it to the base again. My cock was already soaking with the combination of his saliva and my pre-cum. This guy was good.

He spat on my cock, as if it needed anymore lubricating, and deep throated me again.

He gently eased his hands around towards my arse and encouraged me to thrust my cock in his mouth. Gently and rhythmically I bounced back and forth on his throat, his moans increasing the deeper I got.

Part of me wanted him to stop, to savour the moment and feel his tongue explore the rest of my body but he was so good at just doing this that I didn't dare stop him.

I leant back against the doorframe. His mouth was so smooth, and the way he glided over my cock with his tongue was perfect. He now brought his hand into play, sucking me deep and then as his mouth retreated his hand took over. Then mouth, then hand. A master craftsman.

I could feel my cock pulsing and I wanted to reward him with my load. I moaned more loudly as his mouth and hand worked in perfect motion.

"I'm close," I whispered. He moaned and sped up. My cock was soaking wet as he continually went deep with his mouth.

"Oh fuck. Fuck. Fuuuuccck".

I shot and kept on shooting. It just did not stop. I could hear him struggling to take it all in. I went to retreat, out of politeness and concern for his welfare, but he grabbed my arse and pushed my cock right down his throat. He moaned with pleasure as he took my load.

He eventually let my cock go, only to suck it again. He eased my head back over the tip, which dragged a bit more out. He sucked me a little more, until I finally pulled back.

"Fuck. What a load," he gasped.

I pulled my pants up and gave his head a gentle stroke. He laughed and patted my crotch.

I walked out and checked my phone. It had been less than five minutes since I had first entered. I fucking love blowjobs like that. I get some fast and delightful relief, he gets the pleasure of a load down his throat. And who does it hurt? Nobody.

My phone buzzed. It was Matt.

"I've just got home mate. Thanks for a really sweet evening and for cooking. Do it again soon? X"

Yes please.

Chapter Thirteen

A couple of days passed and it was a pretty crisp and cool Saturday morning. I was enjoying a coffee and the newspaper at home.

I exchanged a few messages with the dark room sucker the morning after he had swallowed my load. It turns out that he was visiting with work and renting the flat only briefly. He might return occasionally and would love to suck me sometime. I told him that I would love to drop by again.

I sent Matt a message to see how he was doing.

"Hey Matt, how's your weekend going?"

A few minutes passed without reply so I jumped in the shower. I was feeling quite happy with my body at the moment. I would never describe myself as 'toned' but my gym work was paying off a bit and I carry myself quite well. I'm slim, with a hint of definition. Nothing like Matt, but evidently at least quite appealing to some guys.

I was tall, and taller than the vast majority of guys I hooked up with. I was a bit taller than Matt, who was probably around six foot two. I washed my body and cock in the shower. I was probably about three inches, soft. I trimmed my pubic hair and shaved my balls roughly once a week. I kept my facial hair to a long stubble length. My hair on top was brown and not too dissimilar to Matt's, although his was a bit darker.

I got out of the shower and dried myself. I got into a nice green tee, with a casual green shirt kept open over the top of it. I went for nicely tight black trunks today, with blue jeans and white socks.

I sat back down and saw that Matt was online and had replied to my message.

"Hey! I'm good thanks mate. Just got out of the shower".

Oh, to see him in a towel.

"Nice. Same! What are you up to today?" I replied.

"I'm off to work shortly mate, helping an old colleague move their stuff to their new office. I'm free later on though, and I was actually wondering if you might fancy a drink tonight?"

"That'd be great".

"I want to try this new bar that has live music on a Saturday and apparently decent beers and cocktails. How about we start there?X"

That's right. Matt signed off his message to me with a kiss.

I thoroughly enjoyed our evening earlier this week. My earlier lustful thoughts were clearly still there. I thought him to be fucking beautiful. Not just in his basic physical appearance, although that certainly helped, but his manner too. His cheeky grin floored me.

But there was a softness and warmth that underpinned that. For all that I would happily reflect on the pleasure of him pounding my arse, the truth is that I now cared about him, and how he gradually started to move on and experience intimacy again was interesting to me. I was under no illusions: that intimacy would almost certainly be with somebody else, not me.

And yet the other night *was* intimate. Matt probably hadn't chilled in front of the TV while having somebody casually rub his legs since Emma had done that with him. Just because he didn't stick his tongue down my throat at the end of the night didn't make it meaningless. He was comfortable and happy. I was comfortable and happy.

I have wondered why Matt was so comfortable. A plus of me being a slut is that Matt is probably less concerned about taking advantage. If Matt comes over once in a while and gets a bit touchy with me but doesn't do anything more than that, I'm not going to cry about it. If he gets a bit touchy with me only to then save his actual intimacy and sex for girls, I'm not going to cry.

No. This is good. It feels nice and I'm enjoying this turn of events since I thought he was just a cheeky lad I'd love to get on my knees for.

"That sounds amazing. See you later!x" I replied.

With a kiss.

Chapter Fourteen

I had a productive day of laundry, gym and changing my bedsheets. I was quite grateful for the fact Matt had suggested a live music bar for tonight. As much as I have loved spending time with him so far, we have not actually spent that much time simply talking. The other day there was a movie. The longest conversation we had enjoyed - if that is the right word - to date had been about his widow. To have some live music would be a welcome piece of background to our next encounter.

I reassured myself that there was no need to be nervous and even if there was, worrying about it would only make it harder.

I arrived before Matt. It turned out he had booked us a table that had a nice view of a small stage, which had a tightly packed pianist, percussionist, singer and bass player all combining to play some pretty smooth jazz. It was spontaneous playing rather than individual songs. They were impressive.

Matt arrived a few minutes after me.

"Hey!" He patted me on the shoulder and sat down.

"Hey Matt," I replied. "Nice choice. This bar is amazing".

"Yeah! I'm impressed. I'll go to the bar. What do you fancy to drink, Tom?"

"Ooh. I'll have whatever you're having - surprise me," I said.

Matt was away for a few minutes. It was a busy night and the bar was packed. There were probably around a hundred people here. Lots of groups, but mainly groups of two. Probably couples. Maybe others wondered if we were a couple?

Calm yourself down, Tom.

Matt came back with a bottle of red wine and two glasses.

"Is this okay?" He asked.

"Yes!" I smiled as I replied. "I didn't have you down as a red wine man".

"You shouldn't be so presumptuous about me", Matt smiled too in his reply. He was right.

He poured us each a glass.

"Cheers. To friends and music and doing things again". Matt said.

"Cheers!" We clinked.

The band could continue their entire set in this one long mix of solos, harmonising and soul. It was beautiful. The bass player would get around ninety seconds or so to showcase his talents with only gentle backing from the rest, and then the percussionist would do her thing, the singer their thing then the pianist his. It was exemplary playing. They would also each use their time doing gentle backing as an opportunity to sip a quick glug of beer, wine or whisky, which made us both smile even more.

"This was a really good suggestion, Matt. How come you chose it?" I asked.

"I think it opened the winter before COVID or something like that. Emma had been interested in going. Then obviously everything happened and neither I nor we ever got the chance to go. My mates probably wouldn't enjoy coming to a place like this as a group, and my brother and his wife are a bit too busy being parents. So when the two of us got friendly, it seemed like a good chance to visit".

"I'm flattered. It's a wonderful place," I said.

"Yeah. It is...and I'm off work tomorrow, so let's go wild!"

We clinked glasses again.

"What's your definition of wild?" I asked. He laughed and took another sip of wine.

"To be honest, after the last couple of years I really have no fucking idea. I mean, I love my brother and my sister-in-law and I obviously adore my niece. I am starting to hang out with my mates again, but I don't really know what my social life is right now".

"Well right now it appears to be drinking a bottle of red wine in a romantic jazz bar with a gay", I suggested.

We clinked glasses one last time, this time largely in jest.

We enjoyed the jazz without much conversation for another half an hour or so before they took a well-deserved break. We turned to face each other a bit more instead of the stage.

"Thanks again for coming around the other night. I really enjoyed it," I said.

"No, thank you mate!" He replied. "It was so good to get out of the house and just chill out."

"What did you tell your brother?" I asked.

"About what I got up to? I just told him the truth: that I was going around to a mate's house to watch a film".

"You didn't say that it was a gay friend?" I asked.

"No. I didn't hide it. If he had asked who you were, I would have told him".

"Told him what?" I smiled as I asked.

"That you're a guy that likes massaging calves and cooks a pretty decent chicken". Matt grinned as he replied.

I laughed, and Matt continued.

"No, seriously, I would just tell him who you were and how we met. I don't feel any need to hide who I see or what I do".

"Even to your mate who made those comments about me?" I asked.

"Oh fuck, especially to him! He knows that we have gotten friendly. He has asked me about it, apologised again and it's cool. I don't really think that people like him are inherently homophobic, although I totally understand if you want to call me out on that. I think that they are just ignorant, more than anything. I see it as up to people like me and obviously like you to change that ignorance".

Matt was such an emotionally mature man. I smiled, almost tearfully. I didn't really want to go down a long road of conversation about the importance of allies, but it was great how he spoke.

"Thank you", I humbly offered, smiling at him. "Now, I believe it is my turn to go to the bar. What would you like?".

"Your turn to surprise me mate," he said. "Whatever you're having".

I returned with two espresso martinis.

"If you're having a wild night, you should have some caffeine!" I said, sitting back down next to him.

Matt laughed. "Wow! I have never had one...well, cheers".

We both sipped the joyous mix of coffee, sweetness and strong afterburn of vodka. It was silky smooth with a subtle kick to it. The jazz act kicked back in. This set was a bit more uptempo, with a few more vocal numbers thrown in. A bit of Van Morrison, a bit of Robert Johnson, a bit of musical theatre. It was a perfect accompaniment to the evening.

As we finished the espresso martini, the music was still in full swing. It was now around eleven o'clock.

"Do you want another drink, Matt? And do you want to stay here or go somewhere else?" I asked.

"What would you like to do? What would you normally do?" He asked in reply.

"I would normally head to my favourite gay bar. The one you saw me go to a few weeks ago".

"Are straight guys welcome there?"

"Sure! Anyone is welcome there. Not many straight guys tend to go but not that's not because they're not welcome. Way more straight women go. Hen parties and loud girl groups. I won't lie: I find them quite annoying but it's nice at the same time".

"So I would be more likely to pull than you?" Matt asked.

"You would always be more likely to pull than me".

Matt laughed and shrugged off the compliment.

"Would it be weird for you if I came to a gay bar?" He asked.

"Not weird for me at all," I replied. "I guess I'm just keen to make sure that you're comfortable".

"I expect so," he said. "I think I'm just intrigued to see what the atmosphere is like. I think my mates probably assume it's all orgies and rainbow flags but I'm guessing it's just a nice and friendly vibe except with a bunch of guys rather than being mixed?"

"Yeah, I mean your mates are half right. There's rainbow flags everywhere! Orgies happen in other bars after dark. I promise I won't take you there, don't worry."

"So the bar you would take me to, what's it like?"

"It's just a nice place for a dance and a drink. You won't get a perfectly made espresso martini or a silky smooth red wine like you do here. It's more of a cheap lager, a nasty wine or a basic rum and coke. But ultimately: it's friendly, it's welcoming and it's a safe space to have a good night".

"Okay... I'm game if you are?" He replied.

"Sure?" I asked.

"Definitely!" Matt stood up and was firm. "It sounds fun".

We got ourselves sorted and left the jazz bar, giving a cheery wave and nod to the excellent musicians on stage. We walked for ten minutes or so to get from the jazz bar to the gay bar. The night had definitely gotten colder. There was a real chill in the air. Matt rubbed his hands to keep warm.

We got to the bar and the bouncer recognised me and gave me a hug and a kiss on the cheek. I introduced him to Matt, who gave him a friendly and firm handshake. I laughed and we went inside.

It was full but not super crowded. We couldn't get a seat but we didn't need one. I got us two beers and we stood between the bar and the main dance floor.

"Well, welcome!" I said.

"It's busy! Do you know people here?" Matt asked me.

I scanned the room. I recognised around half a dozen people. One or two friends, plus a few friendly hookups. I gave a friendly wave to a mate who caught my eye.

"Yeah, a few".

"Friends or fucks?"

I smiled. "A mixture".

"I'm not judging by the way," Matt said. "I'm just curious".

"No, it's fine! I won't betray any confidences though. I'm very open about sex in general but I keep the actual people and my experiences with them private," I said.

Matt nodded and smiled.

"Are you feeling alright in here? Your masculinity feels okay?" I cheekily asked.

Matt grinned. My arse twinges when he grins at me like that.

"I'm feeling good," he said. "There is a really nice vibe here. Friendlier than most bars I know".

I passed Matt my beer as I headed off to the toilet. I came back to see that one of my (platonic) friends was talking to Matt.

"Fucking hell," I joked. "I leave you for two minutes and you're already talking to the biggest queer here".

We all laughed and I gave my friend a kiss on the cheek. I remembered that he had been with me a few weeks earlier when Matt had neutralised the homophobic comments from his mate.

"Heyyyyy Tom," my friend said. "Nice to see you. I was just thanking your friend for being an ally, of course. And how do you two gorgeous men know each other?"

I was about to answer when Matt came in first.

"This kind man let me have a piss in his toilet once when I was working in the area, and we just became mates from there".

My friend smiled and was straight back in with his kind-hearted sass. "Oh he lets anybody piss in his area sweetheart, I wouldn't take it as a measure of his kindness".

We both laughed. He gave us both a kiss on the cheek and left.

"He seems nice," Matt said, shouting into my ear as the music was starting to drown us out. We moved to a slightly quieter corner.

"He's an angel," I replied. "Although he's probably off to the sauna as I say that".

"Really? What happens there?"

"What doesn't happen there? You can go there and chill out with a beer and watch some porn, or you can sit in a hot tub, or you can have a private room and fuck somebody, or you can go into the dark area and just let whomever is there do what they like, or you could get your cock sucked at a gloryhole... anything you want so long as it's filthy." I smiled.

"Oh wow. And you've been?" Matt asked.

"No, not really," I replied. "I went to one when I was abroad out of curiosity. Mainly for a walk around. But although I'm quite happily a slut, I'm more into personal and intimate meets. I like the build up of feeling, the vibe I get from someone, the relationship between us. I don't like the randomness of the experience."

"That's the most thoughtful definition of a slut I've heard," Matt joked.

"Probably. Anyway, we have been stationary for too long, mister. Shall we dance?"

Perfect timing, as Erasure's "A Little Respect" blasted throughout the bar. Matt looked so relaxed as he danced his hot little arse off. His hair was quite floppy in the sweaty bar and he was having a great time.

We screamed the chorus together and the music drifted into Abba.

"The tunes are better here than in most other bars!" Matt shouted.

He gave me a hug and he was smiling broadly. He went to the bar and got us another beer. We found a spot that was a bit quieter again and took a break from dancing.

"Cheers! This has been a great night," I said.

A couple of guys came over. I had seen them on the apps before - they're a horny couple and they had chatted to me a few times online. After some pleasantries, they got to the point.

"So we live nearby and we're gonna head home soon. Do you want to come back and chill out with us?" They asked.

"Thanks guys, but we're okay," I replied.

"Hm okay. And how about you?" one of them said, looking at Matt.

"Thanks, but I'm good with this guy. Have a good night guys," Matt replied.

They left, a little disgruntled.

"Nicely handled. I've seen them on the apps - they're fine, just forever horny".

"Yeah. It's fine. How are you feeling by the way? Another drink or do you wanna head home?" Matt asked.

"I'm probably done and ready to sleep soon. Shall we head?" I suggested.

We agreed, drank up and made our way to the door. We live in similar parts of the city so we walked from the bar together.

"It's bloody cold now," said Matt.

He was right. The temperature had definitely dropped and we both had goosebumps on our arms. Thankfully we had our beer, wine and cocktail jackets on.

"The offer is still there if you wanna crash at mine, you know? We could have a nightcap or you can just get some sleep without being woken up early by your niece".

"Haha, she will totally do that. She jumps on my bed every morning if she's up before me".

He was clearly contemplating it.

"You really don't mind?" Matt asked, rubbing his hands together to keep warm.

"Of course not", I replied.

We eventually got back to my flat. It was still quite chilly. I encouraged Matt to make himself comfortable.

"Whisky?" I asked.

"Yeah alright. Thanks."

I brought us both a glass and gave Matt a blanket with which to warm himself. We clinked glasses one last time for the night.

"Thanks Tom," Matt said, "for a really good night. I felt more relaxed tonight than I have in ages".

I joined him on the sofa. "Me too. I had a blast. That jazz bar was amazing".

"The gay bar was great!" Matt exclaimed.

"Ha. The gay bar was a gay bar," I replied. "They're like that every night".

"Do you get propositioned by horny couples every night?"

I smiled. "To be honest, I probably do. But it says more about their horniness than my sex appeal. Gays are horny. Plenty of lads there tonight will spend all night browsing the apps or scanning the room for an arse to fuck. I just like to go out with friends, and I will sort my sex life out in another place at another time".

"When did you last hookup?" Matt asked. "Sorry if that's too personal".

"No, it's fine. Ask me anything. As in, at a bar? Years ago. Before COVID."

"And online?"

I suddenly remembered when it was, and smiled.

"Ha. Well..." I continued. "It was about ten minutes after you left my flat the other night".

Matt laughed, half-choking on his whisky.

"No way! Tell me everything".

I proceeded to tell him some things, but not every little detail. I told him that I was horny, and that a guy nearby was offering me a nice blowjob without anything else wanted in return. And that he had been a man of his word.

"Well fair play mate," Matt said. "It's not for me, but I can see why that's a pretty sweet deal".

I was tempted to ask what *is* for him, but in that moment I did not dare.

"Did you do anything to him?" Matt asked.

"No, it was solely one way," I replied. "He didn't want anything else. It's a common turn on, to give pleasure. I have it a lot".

"You do?"

"Oh god, yes. I don't mean this just sexually. I rubbed your calves last night because I sensed it was nice for you to receive and nice for me to give".

Matt smiled, but stayed quiet. He sipped his whisky. I think we were both a bit reluctant to ask any more sexual questions. I knew it was something that Matt would be comfortable discussing if it was solely about me and my life, but probably not about his own thoughts and feelings. Principally, I suspected, because he maybe didn't even know the answers himself.

I broke the silence. "Don't worry, when all the lights are off tonight I won't get on my knees and blow you".

Matt laughed. "A warm bed will do me. Do you want me to go to bed now so you can nip out and get a nice blowjob from that guy?"

We both smiled.

"I am probably ready for bed to be honest though, Matt. Do you need anything? I have a spare toothbrush that's new, which you can have. I'll get you a towel and a glass of water. Anything else?" I asked.

"No, all good," Matt replied. "Are you absolutely sure that you don't mind?"

"Not at all. It's been nice to have your company. You can get ready first if you like".

He went to the bathroom, a small ensuite next to my bedroom. I nipped into my bedroom to make sure that everything was clean and tidy. I was grateful that I had changed the sheets earlier so that everything was fresh.

Matt came back in, still clothed. Even though he was relaxed and comfortable around me, I could see slight nerves as he wondered what to do and where to go.

"Erm, okay. Which side do you normally sleep on?" Matt asked.

"I usually sleep away from the wall, but you go wherever you like," I replied. "I won't be long".

I went into the bathroom while Matt presumably undressed and got into bed. I had a piss, brushed my teeth and splashed some water on my face. I thankfully didn't smell too sweaty after a long night, and I didn't feel excessively drunk. I don't think Matt did either.

I came back in, and Matt was already in bed on the side against the wall. He had the covers pulled up to his chin, with his hands above the duvet. He looked beautiful. Much though I wish I had been in the room to see him undress, it was just as nice seeing him in my bed. He had a peaceful smile that hinted at the night he had just enjoyed. His hair was very floppy now.

"Hey Tom," he said quietly.

"Hey," I smiled. "I usually sleep in my underwear. Is that okay with you?"

"Yeah that's fine, I'm the same. It is a bit cold though!"

"Sorry, I'll hurry up. You'll soon warm up".

I slipped off my shirt, t-shirt, socks and jeans. Thankfully, I was feeling so relaxed and chilled that I wasn't boasting a boner as I got into bed. Matt looked away out of politeness.

"Have you ever shared a bed with a man before?" I asked.

He paused, as if genuinely trying to remember if he had.

"Not like this," he replied. "Me and my brother did occasionally as kids but that's different obviously. A few shared tents at festivals and stuff, but that's it".

"Cool. Are you feeling okay now? It's one thing being comfortable having a coffee with me, it's another being half-naked next to me. I totally understand if you feel a bit off".

"Thanks Tom, but I genuinely feel fine. I'll be asleep in no time. You've been so cool with me and I feel good. I'm looking forward to warming up and getting some sleep. One thing I'm a little wary about I guess... I don't know what I'm like at night. I might be sound asleep, or I might fidget. Sorry!"

I laughed. "Don't worry, if you end up fidgeting too much I'll kick you. And you can do the same to me".

I turned off the light. Matt spoke in the darkness.

"Goodnight Tom. I think I spend a lot of time thanking you, and sometimes I'm not actually sure why. But thank you mate. Genuinely".

He held my hand tightly.

I gripped it back.

"Goodnight Matt."

Chapter Fifteen

Lying there with my hand in Matt's, I was reminded of those books that I used to read as a child where they give you choices as to what happens next in the story. To enter the cave, turn to page thirty one. To walk around the cave, turn to page thirty five.

What would Matt do if I snuggled into him? What would he do if I kissed him? What would I do if he snuggled into me? I mean, he was already holding my hand...

As it was, Matt didn't hold my hand for long. He let go, touched my arm to signal (and end) his affection, then he turned away from me to get some sleep.

I stayed there lying on my back, both relaxed and a little excited. I had zero expectations as to what might happen here, except in the sense of an expectation that nothing would happen. Yet a week ago I'd never have thought that right now might happen either.

With my mind full of swirling thoughts, my body clock reminded me that it was pretty late and that I had drunk quite a bit. I closed my eyes and eased into a relaxing sleep reasonably quickly.

My memory of what actually happened next and in what order is a little hazy. I think that I slept for about an hour or so and woke up at around two thirty in the morning. Matt was now facing me rather than the wall, but I could see in the low light that he was fast asleep. His legs were curled and bent but he was still firmly on his side of the bed.

I fell asleep again and woke up a couple of hours later to find that I was in bed alone. I quickly wondered if Matt had decided to leave and sleep at home then I heard him pissing and the toilet flushing. He came back in.

"You okay?" I whispered.

"Oh hey. Yeah all good," he whispered back. "Sorry if I woke you up. Fuck it's cold!".

He hopped over me to get into the bed on the wall side, shivering but quickly warming up under the duvet.

"Do you want that dark room blowjob now?" I whispered in his ear.

Matt laughed. "Fuck off and get some sleep".

Matt moved closer to me.

"Can I warm up a bit?" He asked, snuggling in.

"Sure," I whispered in reply.

I lifted my left arm and invited him to snuggle. He rested his head on my chest with one arm around my stomach. His legs stayed separate, whether intentionally to avoid my cock or just incidentally, I had no idea.

He was cold, and I was warm. I kept my left arm near his shoulder and I rubbed his left arm gently with my right.

The next five minutes were heavenly. I could feel Matt getting warmer in my arms. His body felt incredible. His stubble gently scratched my chest. I fought the urge to hold him in a more sensual fashion. I longed to kiss his forehead, to smell him, to run my hand through his hair.

But I didn't. I warmed him up and held him close, and once he had warmed up sufficiently, he placed his left hand on my chest to support himself, moved away from me and settled again on his own pillow.

"Thanks man. Warmer!" he whispered.

I turned away from him to sleep on my side. As I did, his hand affectionately touched and wandered down my back. Almost as if of gratitude. As it reached the bottom of my back, he pulled it away.

We both fell asleep again and when I next woke up it was morning. It was around nine o'clock. I was lying on my back and the sun was just glimpsing through a gap in the curtain.

I looked to my left, and Matt was still asleep facing in my direction. He had a soothed smile on his face. The duvet was up to his neck. His hair had flopped down over his forehead. He looked beautiful and peaceful.

It was at that moment that I felt my erection. I was pretty much rock hard. My cock was leaning towards my left thigh under my trunks.

Delightful though it would have been for Matt to wake up and grab my cock at that exact moment, he stayed fast asleep as I quietly got out of bed and made my way to the bathroom for a shower.

My erection thankfully subsided. I thought about Matt's head resting on my chest. That was nice. Even guys I fuck don't do that with me.

We fuck, they leave.

We fuck, I leave.

We fuck, I piss, they piss, we leave.

Yet here was this guy. No fucking, yet no leaving either.

I dried myself with a towel and wrapped it around my waist. I returned to my bedroom and Matt had woken up and he was sitting up against the headrest.

"Morning," he yawned.

"Hey! How did you sleep?" I asked.

"Good! It's a comfy bed", he replied.

I threw him another towel. "Help yourself to the shower. It's pretty easy to use. I'll make us some breakfast. Do you mind pissing off to the bathroom so I can get changed?"

"Erm... do you mind leaving for a moment while I do. I've woken up with a hard on".

We both laughed.

"Me coming out of the shower has that effect on all the boys," I joked.

I went into the living room, shutting the door behind me. When I heard him shut the door to the bathroom and followed by the sound of the shower running, I nipped back in to get changed: black CKs, a yellow t-shirt and some jeans.

I heard Matt come out of the shower. I knocked, opened the door ajar to speak but not enough to see him naked/semi-naked.

"My pants, socks and t-shirts are all in that wardrobe. Help yourself if you want some clean clothes," I said.

A few moments later, Matt came into the kitchen wearing a white t-shirt of mine. It fit him so much more snugly than it did me.

"Thanks for this mate. And you've made breakfast! I should stay more often", Matt smiled as he spoke.

"Anytime," I replied.

Over breakfast, I thought it okay to ask Matt about sleeping together last night.

"So last night, you've never slept with a guy before yet you quite happily snuggled in for a bit of a cuddle and a spoon. Was that alright with you?"

"Yeah, sorry. Was that ok?" Matt asked.

"Okay with *me*? Mate, I'd happily cuddle the fuck out of you until the end of time. I just want to respect your boundaries," I said.

"Thank you. Yeah, I dunno to be honest. I mean, I was fucking cold! But it was nice".

Matt paused for a moment.

"I don't know that I mean that sexually. Well, I mean. I think that I don't mean it sexually. I've never thought about you sexually. And I don't mean offence by that".

"I know". I smiled at him.

"But," Matt continued, "I enjoyed it. I was comfortable being in bed with you, comfortable in keeping warm close to you, things like that. It's just easy and feels good. And I don't think it's leading you astray. At least, I don't want it to. Sorry, I'm rambling".

"It's not leading me astray. I've no sense you're falling for me or that you have feelings for me". I said.

"But maybe I do have feelings for you", Matt replied.

"Sure. But as a friend," I said.

"Yes, a friend. A mate. But... it is something more than that too. Or at least different to that. It's a feeling I don't have with other friends".

"Okay. That *is* okay, you know?" I touched his arm affectionately. "It's okay to be unsure about something. It's okay to enjoy finding out. You won't hurt me if you choose to find out if you have feelings for me like that and I promise that you won't hurt me if you don't".

"Have you ever had feelings for a woman?" Matt asked

"That's... a very good question." I answered.

It was now my turn to pause.

"Yes. Although, not love. Not really lust either. Just... feelings. She was my best friend when I first started to come out. She's still a friend now to be fair."

"And did you ever sleep with her or do anything?"

"Yeah. We drunkenly snogged a few times at parties. I think she liked me and was maybe a bit frustrated that I didn't feel the same things. Although she didn't love me. We were just young and confused. But we would always share a bed or hang out."

"Did you ever do anything beyond that?" Matt asked.

"She sucked me off a couple of times too," I continued.

"Sure. But any random person can suck you off, right?" Matt joked, referencing my anonymous dalliance the other night.

"Of course", I smiled and bowed my head proudly.

"At this point," I continued, "I had come out to her and I had fooled around with guys a bit. When she asked if I still got turned on by women, I told her that it sort of depends on what they're doing. She started jokingly rubbing my crotch and saw that I got hard. We did that a couple of times and it was fun, but I think she got a bit bored of me and realised it wouldn't be anything more. I wouldn't say that's the same as this".

"So you'd consider yourself gay? Or bi?" Matt asked.

"Yeah gay, but not in any "anti-straight" way. There's maybe a world in which I get to know a hot girl and we click and something happens. Or a world in which a woman turns me on and something happens. It's just that "gay" is an accurate description of what usually clicks for me".

"Yeah, I think I understand you. I've never really spent much time thinking about these things. I was just always straight and then I met someone that confirmed that for me. I didn't look at guys on nights out but to be fair I never really looked at girls either. "Straight" is just an accurate description of my life so far".

"Sure," I said, nodding understandably. "And it's easier for me. I'm open about my sexuality and behaviour. If I want to understand something, I can explore it easily. You've never done that plus you're still mourning. It's not easy".

"I guess". Matt went quiet.

I smiled at him. "More importantly, you do not need to worry one moment about the consequences of placing your head on my chest. It doesn't make you gay or bi or confused or in danger of hurting me. It just means you were cold and my body was warm."

He laughed. "Yeah. I know. I just know I'm in a bit of an odd place now and I don't want to cause you any shit because I'm just unsure with stuff".

"I don't think you need to worry about that. I can't stress to you how comfortable I am in my sexuality and life. If you were to decide to do... whatever with me, only to then find a lovely girl, get married again and have children, I would love to be there celebrating with you. Or, if you want us to never speak again because it would be too uncomfortable, I would understand."

"I hate the idea that I would do that to you", Matt said.

"Well that's your shit, not mine" I said, smiling at him. "You're a good bloke mate. You're allowed to be vulnerable and open and see where the mood takes you, even if it's something you end up changing your mind about. You're also allowed to eat your fucking eggs without depressing us both all morning".

Matt laughed, which was a relief. We ate some eggs, drank some coffee and relaxed a bit more.

"Thank you, Tom. I just have a lot of thoughts going around my head".

"Because you snuggled into me?" I asked.

"Partly. Mainly because I enjoyed it and would like to do it again," Matt replied.

"That's alright, you know?"

"Yeah. Maybe".

"Besides, you're wearing my underwear. That's already turned me on and I'm gonna wank off to that later. I'm in love already and there's nothing you can do about it".

Matt laughed. I was desperate for him to relax about this.

"Okay okay. It's cool! Sorry". Matt said.

"Never apologise for thinking things through openly. That's good and healthy," I replied.

Matt smiled.

"So... Where do we go from here?" Matt asked.

"Wherever we like. It seems you enjoy going for a drink with me and snuggling up when it's cold. If we become good mates and do that once in a while, that'll be nice," I said.

"And if we ever wanted more than that?" Matt asked.

"Well, then we can do that. You can talk to me anytime, or if something just happens sometime I won't judge you".

"And you'd like that?" Matt asked.

"Maybe. If it happened because you were comfortable and wanted it to, then I would probably love that. But ultimately I care about you and respect you, and I respect your mind as much as your sweet little arse".

We both smiled.

"Oh mate," Matt sighed as he drank his coffee. This has been a weird few weeks."

"I know. I know."

"I should probably drift back to my brother's soon. Can we do this again soon? I don't know what I mean by *this*".

"I'd love to".

We finished our eggs, stood up and had our most passionate hug yet. If hugs were penetrative, this hug basically spunked so far up my arse that my nipple leaked.

Chapter Sixteen

Matt texted me a bit later that afternoon. "Thanks again for last night, mate. And sorry for my rambling".

"You really need to stop our conversations being you thanking me and apologising all the time," I replied.

I thought back to my next encounter with Matt. At the very least, Matt might become a hot friend who spoons me. I could not have expected that when he first popped in to use my bathroom.

At the very most... I had no idea.

At the very worst, we both might get hurt. That was easily the outcome of this.

Realising that I was overthinking this as much as Matt was, I got my work things ready for the next day and went to sleep.

I slept well and work itself was uneventful. I went to the gym after work and grabbed some food nearby. I was about to head home ready to welcome Matt around for a snuggle when I got a text. "Hey mate, sorry, can we skip tonight? I'm just not feeling it right now and I'd sooner stay at home".

I walked home, initially feeling a little dejected. I hoped that I hadn't scared him off. I started to wonder if I was just a bit too forward. A bit too slutty. A bit too gay. A bit too... everything.

I soon relaxed. It was pointless for me to tell Matt that it was okay to be confused if I then took issue with him doing just that.

"Hey Matt, of course that's absolutely fine. I hope you're doing alright?x"

I checked in with some friends and they were out for a drink. I decided to join them and I had a nice time, even though I was struggling just a little bit to switch off and enjoy myself.

"I am mate. All good. Just... baby steps haha xx," he replied.

TWO kisses. I smiled and walked home.

Chapter Seventeen

I sent Matt a text the following morning.

"Hey Matt, hope you're doing okay. I'll leave you be and wait to hear from you".

I jumped in the shower then got ready for another day working from home. I sat down at my desk, with no reply yet from Matt.

My day was okay. My doorbell rang for a parcel for Mrs Barnstable in Flat 2. She's never in! She gets more action than me.

After work, and with still no response from Matt, I went for a swim. I hoped that he was feeling okay. I wasn't really sure how I felt at that moment. Part of me was really keen to become his fuckbuddy, his spoon, and his friend. Another part of me was really keen for him to figure stuff out and feel okay. Both of those feelings were rooted in a strong affection for him. Unfortunately, what I didn't know was whether those two feelings were compatible.

As I drifted back home from the pool I logged onto the apps. I had two separate messages, both from old encounters.

The first message read: "Hey mate, we met last week for a dark room BJ. I'm in town again. Fancy popping in later?"

The second message read. "Hey Tom, how's it going?"

The second message was from Anthony, my regular hookup buddy who pounded me the night before my first coffee date with Matt. I replied to him first.

"Hey Anthony, it's okay. A friend is going through a few things and that's on my mind. But good! How are you?" I asked.

"Yeah I'm okay," he replied. "Work has been stressful so I'm just chilling tonight. What are you up to?" he asked.

"Nothing at the moment," I replied. "Dinner then relaxing. What you in the mood for?"

"Wouldn't mind a nice BJ," he suggested.

My mind started running. I suggested to him that we could meet up with a third man; the visiting man who had sucked me off in the dark doorway last week. Anthony was keen. I got back to the other guy.

"Hey mate, welcome back!" I wrote. "I have a mate who fancies a BJ too. Wanna suck us both?"

I sent him our cock pics.

"Fuck, yes please," he replied.

We agreed to a rough time and I told him that I would contact him when we were nearby.

Anthony came around to mine a little later. I met him downstairs in the entrance to my building. We had a quick snog and I felt his crotch. He was already getting quite hard.

"Shall we?" I motioned to the door.

I texted the anonymous sucker to let him know that we were coming and we headed over. Like the last time, the door was unlocked. We walked in, shutting the door behind us. It was dark but there was still a bit of light from the passage window. No whisper from him this time as I knew where to go.

Anthony stuck close to me as we both headed into the room. We saw a shadow by his knees, and sure enough: there he was, waiting.

"Hey guys," he whispered. His left hand moved to my crotch while his right hand moved towards Anthony.

Anthony pulled his jeans down and got his cock out. His cock was around seven inches erect, a nice head with low hanging balls. It really does the job nicely. I couldn't really see what happened next except that a shadow was going straight in and deep to Anthony's dick.

Anthony moaned much like I had the other day. He looked at me and kissed me passionately. I kissed him while my hand gently massaged the back of the sucker's head. His mouth came off Anthony's dick and he seemed to enjoy two guys kissing above him.

"Fuck yea. That's hot guys," he said.

The third man moved over to me, undoing my belt and pulling down my jeans and underwear. We both now had our pants around our ankles. I stroked Anthony's cock while the gent sucked me deep.

The third man started sucking me deep in one motion, slowly retracting then swiftly sucking Anthony deeply. He gracefully went from one cock to the other, each time going that little bit faster.

I was feeling horny and in the mood to shoot. "I wanna shoot down your throat," I said.

The third man moaned and started to quicken his motions. Anthony walked around and stood wide-legged over the third man's head and started kissing me. The gent's hands roamed Anthony's legs behind him while his mouth went deeper and faster on my cock.

My groans hinted at the inevitable outcome that was about to follow, and within a few seconds I was shooting down the third man's throat. Anthony's tongue was down my throat and my heavy breathing went right through him as I shot my load.

Anthony stopped kissing me and moved back around to stand next to me while the third man's throat finally let go of my cock.

He got straight to work on Anthony. Meanwhile, I got behind Anthony and got on my knees. I rubbed his thighs and his arse, teasing his perineum with my fingers.

Anthony was clearly enjoying himself. My eyes were starting to adjust to the light a little and I looked between Anthony's legs to see that the third man was wanking. His cock was small but looked rock hard.

Anthony's arse and legs were thrusting his cock into the third man's mouth. It was so hot to sit underneath and watch it back and forth.

His thrusting got faster and I could feel his legs starting to shake. The third man moaned and I saw him shoot his load over the floor in front of him. A few seconds later, Anthony withdrew his cock and wanked his load out over the third man's face. I couldn't make out his face in great detail but I could see the dribbling cum.

I stood up and gently kissed Anthony's neck. We both put our hands on the gent's head and thanked him.

"Thanks lads. Come back anytime," he said.

We pulled our pants up and made our way out.

"You doing alright, Tom?" Anthony asked me. "What's going on with that mate you mentioned?"

I checked my phone, and there was still no message from Matt.

"Oh it's fine mate. It's a bit private. Just a friend who is having a tough time", I said.

"Okay. Well I hope you both get sorted".

I gave Anthony a hug and we went our separate ways. I got home with some post-spunk cum dripping in my pants. I thought about texting Matt but my slutty wisdom was probably not what he needed right now.

Chapter Eighteen

A few days went by. It was now Friday evening and I had not heard from Matt all week. I decided not to worry too much about it.

I couldn't really put myself in his position. I have next to no hesitation when acting on mutual sexual and physical desires. I also usually have no hesitation about making up my mind about what those desires are. For example, when an anonymous man - like the third man from the other night - tells me he's on his knees in a dark room waiting to suck me off, I'm very relaxed in quickly deciding if that's something I want to do or not.

Matt isn't in that position. Whether because he has so many thoughts swirling around his head or just because he's a bit unsure, I don't know. Does he want to do anything with me? Or am I merely the first person that's actually provided an outlet for him to think about these things in a long time?

There are guys like Matt that pop up on the gay apps all the time. Their circumstances are different - they're usually cheating on a partner, or not out, or just visiting and sensing an opportunity to do something they cannot do at home - but the way they dither or worry is often the same. With those guys, I have no bond and after a little while of trying to "woo" them, I give up if it's complicated. I don't need the hassle.

With Matt, it's different. I have the bond now. But as much as I might long to hold him, kiss him and blow him, I did not want to cause him worry or drama or confusion.

I want that cheeky grin back on his face more than anything.

I was staying in tonight and chilling on my own with some TV. I wouldn't say I was moping - I had had a busy week and just wanted to chill out - but nonetheless I could have been a little bit happier than I was.

I browsed the apps occasionally through the night and chatted to a few friends with benefits there, but ultimately I wasn't really in the mood for a meet tonight. I thought about texting Matt to check that he was okay, but he knew where I was and knew that I was here if he wanted or needed me.

It was around eleven o'clock when I decided to head to bed, hoping to get some sleep and have a productive Saturday of gym, laundry and shopping. I got into bed and my phone buzzed.

"Hey Tom. How are you?X" It was Matt.

"Nice to hear from you. I'm doing alright. How are you?" I replied.

"I'm alright. I'm sorry I've not been in touch. I've had a busy week at work and stuff at home and I just needed a bit of space to actually do as you suggested and relax!"

"That's good! I'm glad to hear it. And do you feel better for it?"

"I do mate. I'd love to see you soon if you're around?" He asked.

"Yeah okay that sounds great. What are your plans over the next few days?"

There was a brief pause in communication. Then Matt again.

"I was wondering if I could come over now?X"

"I've just got into bed..." I wrote, and continued. "If you like, you're very welcome to come over and stay with me?"

"If that's ok, I'd love that mate," he replied.

Oof. I was surprised to hear from him, and especially to hear from him in such a definite and confident way. But my head, heart and cock all told me it would be fine.

"Okay then. Come on over x"

Chapter Nineteen

About fifteen minutes later, my doorbell rang. Upon hearing that it was Matt, I buzzed him up. I held the door open in my underwear. I was quite relaxed about this and ultimately we were going straight to bed.

I saw Matt come up the stairs. He looked as stunning as ever in a white tee, black jeans and white trainers. He had had a haircut and it was very nicely short and spiky.

"Hey Matt".

He came in and removed his trainers to show some white ankle socks. I suddenly realised I was very quickly in danger of having a hard on in front of him.

"Tom, hey mate".

He gave me a hug - fuck's sake Matt, not the best way to help my erotic thoughts subside - and held me tightly. He seemed relieved to see me.

"How are you, Matt? It's so great to see you".

"Yeah mate, I'm alright. I had a worried and troubled couple of days and I gradually just realised that actually it's not important or worth the trouble of worrying."

"That's good!" I replied. "Do you want a drink or anything or do you actually want to get to bed?"

"Well, I mean you're currently freezing your arse off in your underwear mate, so maybe let's get straight to bed?" He suggested.

We both smiled and agreed. Matt had a backpack with him, including his own toiletries this time. He had planned ahead.

I got us some water, got into bed while Matt went to the bathroom. I smiled as I reflected upon how many times I had now heard Matt pissing in my toilet.

Matt came back out and smiled at me as I sat in bed.

Matt took off his shirt. For all the time we'd spent together, this would be the most I'd ever actually "seen" him standing in the flesh. His upper body was just perfect to me. He clearly worked out and he was quite naturally toned anyway, and it just suited him. Right now, it suited me too.

He had a tuft of hair between his pecs and a nice little trail underneath his belly button, which ever so slightly popped in. He had a hint of a six pack and a very definable chest.

He took off his jeans to reveal sky blue trunks. They were tight and they rested quite high up his thighs, which were a little bit hairy although not as hairy as mine. He took off his socks and joined me in bed.

"Last time we were the other way around," Matt said. "No matter".

I looked at him as we both sat up, our heads turned to face the other.

"I don't want to ask how you're feeling just for the sake of it, but if you want to talk or if you want to just sleep I don't mind either way", I said.

Matt smiled. "All good mate. I'm feeling happy about this. I don't know exactly what I want to happen but I know I'm happier here than not here. Shall I get the light?"

I smiled, affectionately held his arm, and Matt turned the light off.

My room doesn't let lots of light in but it isn't perfectly dark either. The anonymous third man would not feel sufficiently discreet to suck cock here. I lay on my back, glancing rightwards towards Matt, who I could see was nestling down.

Matt smiled at me and said, "Turn over if you like".

I turned to face the wall, my back to Matt. His right arm came over as he spooned into me. I had to fight not to groan with pleasure. This felt so nice. His arm rested under mine and fell across my chest and his hand settled on my stomach. I felt his chest and stomach fall into the crevices and dips of my back. His legs bent seamlessly into mine. I could feel his gentle breathing on the back of my neck.

You know those moments where things just slot in perfectly into position? The final brick into a wall. The book that slots neatly among the others into a shelf. Matt's body was now perfectly in place alongside mine. I wanted to tell him how nice this felt, I wanted to moan and nestle in more, but that he was doing this and it felt good was something I decided just to lie down and enjoy.

Matt gripped me tightly and nestled in a bit further. I loved that he wanted to do this with me. I held his arm as it spooned me.

Matt kissed me on my shoulder. It took me by surprise and I moaned gently.

"Hey," he whispered in my ear. I whispered the same back.

He kissed me again on the shoulder. His hand wandered around my arm and chest. I went to nestle my head further into the pillow when Matt released me and pulled my shoulder back to the bed so that I was now lying on my back.

I looked into his eyes. He had that grin on his face. I would call it romantic, but I think we all know by now that its main effect was to leave my cock dripping.

Matt kissed me.

It was solely lips. No tongue. A kiss that suggested he wasn't fully sure of what he wanted. But still, FUCK FUCK FUCK Matt was in my bed and kissing me. His kiss held my lips for a few seconds then he pulled away and looked into my eyes.

"Hey," he smiled.

I smiled back.

He looked at me, a little uncertain. I pulled his face back towards mine and kissed him. He moaned gently as my tongue gently caressed his. I held the back of his head with my left hand, his hand with my right. He gradually settled into kissing me, the way that any two people kissing for the first time need to figure out how to do.

He gently eased his tongue a little further and quite quickly he was relaxed as he sat up over me. His right hand wandered around my chest and settled on my stomach.

Matt sighed happily and sat up.

I smiled. "You feeling okay?"

Matt looked at me, with a beaming grin.

"Are you serious? I feel great! I don't know necessarily what I want to do but this is great".

"That's alright". I smiled. "We can just explore and see how we feel".

"What do you like to do?" Matt asked me.

"Whatever keeps you grinning like that", I replied.

Me simply saying that to him elicited the facial reaction for which I was hoping.

"So you enjoy giving pleasure?" He asked.

I nodded, almost moaning and my cock almost throbbing just for him asking that.

"God yes. If I turn you on, I'm turned on".

Matt lay down and rested his head on the pillow. I moved up off my back and climbed on top of him. I decided to stop asking if he was okay. He would show me if he wasn't, and right now any sense of nerves he had felt had long gone. My body gently glided across his while we kissed passionately.

I straddled him, sitting on his stomach while my legs rested on either side, and looked down at his face and body.

"You are truly beautiful, you know that?"

Matt went shy. I gently stroked his body with my hands. As my hands passed over his nipples, he moaned loudly, almost as if surprising himself.

"Oh fuck", he blurted out.

"Wow. Your nipples are VERY sensitive".

"Yeah... I knew they were but that was intense".

"That's hot... close your eyes", I said.

I placed my right forefinger on his right nipple and gently moved it around. He moaned again. Then my middle finger, then my third, then finally my little finger. I gently flicked his nipple with my forefinger. He moaned ever more loudly.

I hovered my hand over his right nipple without touching it. I held it there for a few seconds, and he gradually started to open his eyes.

"Keep them closed," I leant down and whispered.

I let five or ten seconds go by where I was so close to touching but ultimately not touching his nipple. Then I brought my fingers together and massaged it with the palm of my hand. He jolted up with pleasure.

"Oh my god", he moaned.

I kneeled down and kissed him. He moaned and kissed me with the warmth of a man enjoying himself. I moved down and licked his right nipple now and he moaned even more. Every time he moaned he looked surprised and embarrassed at his inability to keep his noises in check.

"Nobody's ever done this to me", he said.

I smiled. I continued to lick his right nipple with the occasional little playful nibble.

"Close your eyes again," I said.

I sat back up. As I did so, I could feel his dick throbbing under my arse.

Until now, I had ignored his left nipple. His right nipple had received a few minutes of pleasure and teasing while his left nipple had been left all alone. I took my forefinger and placed it gently in Matt's mouth. He moaned and licked it. I then placed my finger over, on and around his left nipple.

"Oohhhhh fuck mate," Matt moaned, groaned, laughed and grinned in equal measure.

I went straight down and vigorously licked his left nipple then his right, sweeping between the two as he moaned and gasped.

I eventually stopped to let him breathe. Matt leant up and kissed me.

I rubbed his entire chest with my hands to calm him down and gradually ease his intense reactions back down to more manageable levels.

"You're so fucking sexy," I said. Matt smiled at me and lay back to enjoy my work.

I gradually moved down to his stomach and kissed around his abs. I looked down to see his hard on through his trunks. I looked up and smiled at him.

I moved to his legs. He really was just perfect. His legs were popping out of his trunks. I massaged his thighs, much like I had his calves when we'd watched the film recently.

"Your hands feel really nice mate," he said.

"I love giving massages. We can do that properly sometime if you like" I replied. He nodded weakly.

I moved his legs wide so that I was now on my knees between his legs. His calves came back in to wrap around my body. I massaged his thighs from his knees to his underwear. I gradually moved ever closer up his thighs and ever more towards the inside. His legs had a nice amount of hair to them, less than mine but more than many of the gym-fit guys that shave or wax them.

I could see his cock twitching under his pants.

"You doing alright in there?" I smiled, looking at his crotch.

"Yeah... this is all quite intense. In a good way!"

I pulled his pants off. He brought his legs up so I could remove them past his legs. He was pretty flexible and his legs went high up, enough that I saw underneath his balls and a brief glimpse of his hole before I eventually saw his cock. I threw his pants to the floor.

Matt looked beautiful naked.

His cock was smaller than mine. I would guess that it was just a little under six inches and he was pretty much fully erect. Thankfully, I've never been obsessed with size. So many guys message me on the apps boasting about their big cock. I mean sure, that's great. But is it a nice one?

Matt's was a very nice one. He was uncut with his head just nicely covered by his foreskin. It was beautifully veiny, with balls hanging nicely but not too lowly. Everything was just nicely proportioned.

I returned to his thighs, but this time with my mouth. My lips worked their way up his thighs. Matt found it hard to lie still as my mouth moved ever closer to his cock.

"You're fucking unbearable," Matt said, openly laughing as he did so.

I smiled and moved my tongue to his balls. Matt moaned. My tongue explored each of his balls. They had a little hair but he clearly took some care of them. Above his cock was a nice little bed of pubic hair. I moved just under his balls with my tongue to his perineum. Matt moaned loudly and again gave the impression he was experiencing sensations he hadn't experienced before.

"I don't know that I want you to go lower". Matt said.

I smiled. "That's okay, I won't".

I decided to go higher instead. His perineum could wait. My tongue slowly went up his cock. As I reached the tip, there was a mountain of precum dripping. I soaked it up and took Matt's cock in my mouth. Matt groaned and ran his hands through my hair as my mouth wrapped around his dick.

It felt beautiful in my mouth. My tongue felt each vein throbbing and eventually that glorious feeling of a fully hard cock hitting the back of my throat.

My mouth slowly moved up and down his cock. The combination of pre-cum and my saliva made him so deliciously wet. I was looking forward to savouring this for a while. Until I got a very immediate sense that I might only be enjoying it briefly.

"Oh shit mate, stop", he said.

I felt his veins throbbing and his cock pulsing: that wonderful feeling of somebody about to shoot a hot load. There were two options at this exact moment. Matt could either come prematurely feeling pointlessly bad and guilty; or I could help him to embrace it and insist that he shoot his load right down my throat right now.

I opted for the latter.

I moaned warmly to signal how much I wanted to swallow his load and even if he wanted me to stop, I wouldn't let him. I grabbed his hands in mine and held them tightly as my mouth sped up. I moaned loudly while his cock filled my mouth. I could not wait to taste him.

"Fuck. Mate. Oh mate. Oh fuck, I'm gonna cum".

He shot. And shot. And shot. It felt like it would never stop. I gleefully took and swallowed it all.

Matt smiled and looked exhausted.

"Oh my god. Sorry Tom. I didn't want to come that quickly".

I slowly released his cock, which was still hard. I swallowed the last drops in my mouth and kissed the tip of his cock.

"Matt, never ever apologise for shooting down my throat. That was hot".

"It's been a while..." he said.

"I could tell", I smiled.

I gave Matt his pants to put back on so that we could get some snuggle back together.

"What do you think you're doing?" Matt asked.

"That was amazing. Let's get some sleep?"

Matt laughed. He was still hard.

"Mate, I'm not ready to sleep. It's your turn now."

"But..."

"I'll spunk again, don't worry about that".

Fuck. My cock throbbed hearing that.

"I would kiss you but of the many things I'm wondering if you're ready for, tasting your own spunk maybe isn't one of them".

We laughed, and I kissed Matt on the cheek. I went to the bathroom and rinsed my mouth out.

I came back, and Matt's cock had softened but only a little.

"I love how you stay hard," I said.

He got out of bed, stood up next to me and kissed me.

"I want to do other things with you but I don't really know what those things would be," he said with a hint of embarrassment.

I smiled. "That's alright. We don't need to do absolutely everything. You have just kissed a lad, had your nipples teased by a lad and you've just shot a load down my throat. They're hardly baby steps anymore!"

He laughed. "Yeah fair point". We both lay down on the bed. "What would you want me to do to you then?"

"You can just explore my body and play with me in any way that you want."

He pulled my pants down and saw me naked for the first time.

"Fair play mate!" He said, looking at my cock.

My cock is bigger. It's around seven inches. I don't think that it is quite as nice as Matt's cock, but it's similarly uncut, with a bit more hair trimmed away.

He grabbed it, a little cack-handendly but I wasn't an expert cock handler the first time I did it either.

"Just be gentle and enjoy whatever you do", I suggested. He held my cock in his hand and gently played with my balls with his left.

"Is that okay?"

I nodded.

His left hand drifted a little lower. I spread my legs wide to allow him to go a little lower. His left hand massaged my perineum and occasionally wandered close to my hole.

"Is that okay?"

I nodded, smiling. He began to gently rub my hole with his left hand while he slowly wanked me with his right. He spat on his left hand, and returned to hovering over my hole. I moaned. My hole was easily my most sensitive area.

Matt smiled. He was enjoying the pleasure he was providing. His cock was rising again. He leant in to kiss me.

The more Matt played with my hole, the wetter my cock got.

"Fuck, you're dripping," he noted.

"I'll be shooting if you keep doing that," I noted in reply.

"Do you like your hole being played with?"

I nodded. "I love it."

"Maybe I could fuck it sometime"?

My cock throbbed in his hand as he said that. Matt grinned at me.

"I think you're enjoying being in control," I said.

As I did, Matt eased a finger ever so slightly into the edge of my arse. I moaned and dripped some more.

"Maybe," he smiled.

He let go of my cock and hole and moved up my body to stick his dick in my mouth. I angled my body so that I was in a better place to get my mouth fucked. He looked down at me, knees either side of my shoulders, to see if this was alright. I nodded pleadingly. I grabbed his arse cheeks to beg him to fuck my throat.

He quickly pounded my throat while my hands massaged his arse cheeks. I managed to reposition my left hand so that it reached up to play with his nipple. He groaned. I wanked myself with my right hand.

"Fuck that's nice," he said, grinning. Matt's cock was leaking again. Is this still pre-cum? Post-cum? Soon it would be another shot of cum and I wanted it.

Matt more aggressively pounded me in such a way as to suggest that if he did pound my arse sometime then I was definitely in for a treat. As I angled down to suck him more effectively, I couldn't reach his nipple anymore but that didn't bother him. He had his hands on the bed stand to angle himself into an essentially missionary position. He was pounding my throat dominantly.

"God Tom, I'm getting close again".

I moaned loudly, partly to indicate my enjoyment but also to hint that I was about to shoot too.

I went first and felt a hefty load release. I later discovered that it had hit Matt's back. I groaned and tried to get some air into my lungs in any way that I could, all the while gratefully pleading longingly for his load with my moans. This combination of my spunk and my begging got him very excited and this was his cue.

"Oh fuck, I'm gonna come".

For the second time in a short while, he filled my mouth. There was understandably less of it this time, but he still shot a fair load down my throat. He collapsed his hands off the bed stand to my chest and took his cock out. He collapsed again to lie on top of me. If my spunk wasn't dripping down his back, we could have fallen asleep right there.

"You okay?" I asked.

He nodded weakly. "That was nice".

He quickly hopped up and ran towards the shower as fast as he could to avoid cum dripping everywhere. I ogled as his cheeks gently wobbled away with his balls hanging ever so slightly underneath.

I decided to leave him to shower alone first. For all the erotic stories of shower sex and intimate moments, I generally found it a bit of an uncomfortable experience and I was happy to give him a minute to catch his breath and for me to catch mine.

As I joined, he was washing the shower gel suds away.

"Is my back clean?"

He grinned at me and invited me in.

"Yes!" I replied, stroking his shoulders.

He held me and kissed me. Even allowing for my hatred of intimate shower moments, I had to admit that this was quite sweet.

He hopped out of the shower and brushed his teeth while I washed myself. He left and headed back to bed as it was my turn to brush. As I returned, he was in bed and now closest to the wall.

"Thank you mate", he said. "I had to fight some insecurities to come here tonight but I'm so glad I did".

"Me too. Now, fuck off", I replied, jumping into bed and stretching out across him.

Matt grabbed my crotch and laughed. "Nope! You're all mine, now".

Fuck. A lot had happened tonight.

"Good night, Matt".

"Good night, Tom".

I got the light, Matt turned away from me and grabbed my arm to spoon around him. We both fell asleep in an instant.

Chapter Twenty

I was alone in bed - Matt must have already woken up. My jaw happily ached a little from the oral pounding he had given me a few hours earlier. I shuffled up to rest my head against the headrest. Matt heard me and came in from the living room.

"Morning mate". He said, handing me a coffee.

"Hey! How are you feeling?" I asked.

"Good! Dick is a little tender but otherwise good".

"Well you will fuck my mouth and come twice" I pointed out.

"You might be right," he smiled as he replied.

He went in to give me a kiss. I stopped him. He looked crestfallen.

"Sorry... what's wrong"? He asked innocently.

"There are many things I want you to discover with me. Morning after cum-breath combined with black coffee is absolutely not one of them".

He laughed, and pushed my head away affectionately.

"I've already showered. You were dead to the world! How about you shower and we go get some breakfast somewhere?" Matt suggested.

I drank my coffee, brushed my teeth and jumped in the shower. I had wondered if Matt might feel regretful the morning after. Even if he had taken some time to think things through this week, he had also come over very spontaneously. Yet there he was in my living room, all smiles and full of the joys of a double cum-shot.

"Now can I kiss you?" Matt asked, as I entered the living room now fully dressed.

I walked up to him and kissed him gently on the lips. Gradually, our tongues found each other and he placed his left hand on the back of my head and his right hand on my arse. I slapped him away playfully and we headed out for breakfast.

We walked for about ten minutes to a nearby cafe. En route we passed the flat of the third man: the anonymous gentleman from a few days prior.

"Do you remember that dark room blowjob I mentioned?" I asked.

"Yes", Matt laughed as he responded.

I pointed to a flat across the road.

"Oh!" said Matt. "Very convenient. How many times have you been there?"

"A couple. Once on my own, another time me and a mate went together. He's just a good sucker. Nice and easy."

"You really are relaxed about all this stuff, aren't you?" He asked.

"Yeah. Is that okay?"

"Of course it is. I'm just adjusting a bit".

We smiled and carried on walking to the cafe in relative silence. We sat down and got a couple of full English breakfasts to reward our intense efforts from the night before.

"When I say I'm adjusting..." Matt spoke, munching on some baked beans as he did so, "I guess I just admire how open you are and I wish that I was like that. But I'm not really like that and I don't know if I'm happy or jealous about that".

"To be fair", I replied, "you coming around last night and doing what you did was very open. I had not expected it".

"That's true... I guess if you ever had similar feelings for a woman you would act on them?" He asked.

I paused to think about that for a second, but I already knew my answer. "Yes, definitely. As I've said before, I'm gay but if I ever had that sense of attraction to a woman, I'm sure I would act on it quite comfortably. It's to your credit that you did the same, and to your credit that you don't regret it this morning".

"I definitely don't regret it! If anything, I want to do it again and more of it."

I smiled.

"Well that makes me and my cock very happy indeed".

Matt laughed. "How did... how did I do? I know I didn't do much to you".

"You didn't need to. But what you did was very hot. Do you think you may have feelings for other guys like that in the future, or was it an individual thing with me?"

Matt sighed. "I've no idea to be honest, mate. I'm just trying to stay relaxed about it. I'm not that bothered about seeing your anonymous cock sucker friend, put it that way".

"His loss", I smiled.

"But I do want to do more things with you Tom, even if I'm just sure what they are".

"That's cool. Plenty of time to explore. It's probably good if you take it slowly. Even taking these things slowly, it can be a bit overwhelming".

Matt nodded. "That's true. I'm a bit wary of being a bit full on or strong. And I don't want to encroach on your own circumstances mate", he continued. "I know you do other things with other people, and I want to be alright with that".

"Thank you," I said, smiling. "The same to you: if this leads to you wanting to shag a girl or to see another guy or whatever, please please please do that. Just... tell me about it in great and vivid detail when you do".

We laughed.

"Maybe," he said. "I don't know."

"Was it what you expected? Did you expect anything?" I asked.

"It felt much more comfortable than I expected," he said. "I thought I would be nervous... and I still was a bit. I mean... I came prematurely..."

"That was hot though. I never understand why people panic too much about that. I've shot early a load of times."

"Yeah... I guess I made up for it the second time! But yeah, I didn't have any expectations. I just hoped I would enjoy it, which I did. And your mouth... jesus mate, I enjoyed that".

I smiled. "Can I ask about your sex life with Emma?"

"Sure. It was good, but we were both virgins when we got together, to be fair. It was hot, but mainly hot because of how horny we were for each other rather than any fantastic technique. I don't think she physically enjoyed sucking me, for example. You on the other hand...".

We both smiled.

"Yeah. I really enjoy giving pleasure. It's a turn on to turn a guy on".

"I enjoyed playing with your cock too," he continued. "I hope I wasn't too rough or too gentle".

I laughed. "Not at all. Lots more still to enjoy in time."

"Thanks mate," he replied. "And I don't want this to just be some learning journey for me. I want you to enjoy it".

I smiled. "I can promise you that I will. I really fucking enjoyed last night. Kissing you and feeling you relax, and then by the end of the night you fucking my throat... I enjoyed it all a lot".

Chapter Twenty One

Matt texted me later that afternoon. He thanked me again for last night and we arranged to meet again the following evening. That night, I had a great time out in the gay bars with some friends and my head felt quite delicate the morning after. I had a lazy Sunday morning and then went for a swim in the afternoon.

Matt came over that evening after dinner. He had his tightest jeans on with a black t-shirt. He hugged me and came in.

"Hey," I said. "I'm gonna have a hard time getting your legs out of those".

He laughed. I got us a beer and we sat down on the sofa. I had the TV on but it was very much in the background.

"How was your day?" I asked.

"Yeah good. I was delivering today. No young naked women or guys in their underwear, unfortunately! But all good, mate. My brother asked me who I was spending my time with."

"What did you tell him?" I asked.

"I said that I'd become friends with a guy locally. I think he just assumed you were straight. He asked how we'd met and I said I'd delivered a few parcels and just got chatting and that we'd gone to the music bar that time."

"Did you mention that you shot two loads down this friend's throat the other night?" I asked.

"I did not". He gently and teasingly kicked me.

"Did he have any comments?"

"Not really. I think they're just a bit relieved I'm doing things again and feeling alright."

I smiled. He leaned over to me and kissed me.

We snuggled in and we watched some TV. As the evening went on, our hands started wandering around each other. His head rested on my chest and his hand rested on my crotch.

"How do you feel when you touch me?" I asked.

"Good, although maybe a bit weird too. Part of me doesn't know what I want to do. Part of me thinks I might know what I want to do but then I don't know what you want. But that excites me. And then I don't know what else you will do to me".

"That sounds a bit threatening..."

"Maybe I like that," he grinned as he replied.

I asked him to stand up and I got onto my knees. I unzipped his jeans and pulled them down (as best as I could - they were tight).

"Maybe I like this," I said.

His cock was already semi-hard. It flopped out beautifully and almost landed straight onto my tongue. His head was already slightly naturally pulled back.

I took his cock into my mouth and felt it grow instantly. His cock was perhaps slightly smaller than average, but it felt perfect. Beautifully veiny, a head that just pulled slightly back, and balls that hung a little bit below, and so evidently full and ready to shoot everywhere.

"Fuck, mate. That's nice". Matt turned off the TV and gently caressed my hair with his hand as I slowly took his cock deeper and deeper in my mouth.

His cock was now fully hard and dripping on my tongue as I slowly went back and forth. He grabbed my head a little bit more vigorously and guided it a bit more so as to suit his own sensations. He was getting more and more confident and comfortable with me.

I gradually moved lower. My tongue caressed his balls. I gently went firmer with my tongue as I tried to sense how sensitive his body was here. I personally don't enjoy my balls being aggressively played with. Other guys love it. He seemed to enjoy my mouth being more aggressive.

I took one of his balls in my mouth, keeping it in my mouth while my tongue rolled vigorously over it. He moaned loudly. I took both balls now in my mouth and he moaned even more. He breathed heavily while forcing my head further into his crotch with his hand.

I looked up and Matt was looking right down at me. He had a wide smile on his face and a fucking beautiful glint in his eye. I moaned loudly. Matt was surprised and softened his grip on my head.

"Are you okay?" He asked.

My mouth was full and all I could was moan louder to signal my enjoyment rather than my discomfort. He smiled again. I slowly wound down my play of his balls and gradually released them from my mouth.

My tongue went a little lower to his perineum. I don't think that Matt is ready for me to rim him yet, but he is definitely ready for this. My tongue gently roamed around underneath his balls, making soft and circular motions.

"Oh. Wow." Matt breathlessly muttered as he tried to comprehend what he was feeling.

I was now directly underneath him as my tongue worked across his perineum. I was so turned on at providing him with this new sensation. My hands massaged his legs.

"This feels really fucking nice", Matt said. "I still don't think I want your tongue going any lower".

I smiled and moved back slightly to face him.

"That's okay! If you feel comfortable another time we can try it. Or never: it's fun only if that's how it feels."

I quickly put my tongue back where it was and drifted between his balls and his perineum. He moaned and was almost knocked a bit off his feet. He pulled me up to standing next to him and kissed me passionately.

"Can I ask a question?".

"Sure," I replied.

"How often do gay guys fuck? Always? Never? Who does what?"

I smiled.

"It depends on the guy. Some people only fuck. Some people only get fucked. Some people never do either. Some people mix it up. It's just about understanding and communicating really".

"That's cool. And how about you mate?"

"I mix it up. I'm what's known as versatile. I fuck and get fucked. But it's not everything for me. Sex is more than just a good pounding."

"But it helps?" Matt grinned as he asked.

"Yes. Sometimes it helps".

"And how easy do you find it?"

"Nowadays, it's much easier. It takes time and patience, and a considerate guy who respects that. And lube. Lots of lube, Matt".

"I loved seeing your face as I touched your arse the other day", said Matt.

I smiled. I kissed him. I took his clothes completely off, grabbed his hand and pulled him towards my bedroom.

I stripped naked and stood in front of him. We were both completely naked now. He smiled, although a little unsure of what might happen next.

I turned around and got on to bed, face down. I turned my head around to see him smiling at me.

"Just take your time and explore me, if you like. Don't worry about doing anything wrong. Just feel me, have a poke and a stroke around. There's lube there if you want to go any further, and I'll tell you if there's anything I don't want to happen".

Matt took a deep breath. "Okay! Let's do this".

Matt got on top of me so he was straddling my legs. I felt his cock - still hard - gently tap my left thigh. His hands gently massaged my arse cheeks. I gently moaned and settled into the pillow.

"Is this okay?"

"Very okay. Just enjoy yourself".

"What, like this?" He asked.

He gently spanked me. I moaned loudly, caught by surprise.

"Oh fuck. Yeah, just like..."

He spanked me again, harder.

"Fuck! Yes, like that". I breathed heavily, feeling the sensations running through my body.

Matt laughed, gently massaging my arse once more. "Okay okay. I'm getting the hang of this".

As he continued to massage my arse, he got closer to my hole with every motion. He leant down and kissed my cheeks. I widened my legs to give my assurance that this felt good.

There was a pause. I hoped that he was feeling okay.

Then I felt his tongue glide over my hole...

Chapter Twenty Two

"Oh my god". I grabbed the corners of my bed. "Fuck, yes".

Matt briefly took his head away from my hole to gauge my reaction. Upon seeing it was hot, he dived straight back in.

His technique wasn't perfect. He didn't teasingly build me up. Do you remember that scene in Queer As Folk? The tongue begins at the top of the back. Then it drifts slowly and seductively down to the middle. Then the tongue gradually goes down into the valley-like crevices of the lower back, before it finally nestles on that peachy hole.

Well, imagine the opposite of that. Matt was tongue fucking my hole, and quite roughly as his stubble scratched my skin as his tongue freely drifted around.

But I did not need perfect technique. Because Matt. Beautiful Matt. Gorgeous Matt. Matt was rimming my arse on my bed, in my bedroom, and I was really fucking enjoying it.

He spanked my arse again.

"I quite like your arse," Matt said, coming up for breath. I could hear in the way he said it that he was grinning.

"I think you're quite enjoying treating me like a little bitch," I breathlessly said in reply..

Matt laughed. "I'm not so sure about that." He spanked me again. "But then again, maybe I am..."

I laughed at the same time as Matt buried his tongue back into my hole. It's a wonderful feeling to be both giggling and so immensely turned on that you physically cannot help but writhe around on the bed. He gently spanked my arse one last time and sat up.

"How was that?" He asked, with a beautiful innocence.

"Fucking hot mate. Did you enjoy it?"

"Yeah! I dunno how good I was. I used to love eating Emma out. Hope you don't mind me saying that".

I shook my head. "It's hot mate. Share whatever you want to share".

"I loved it but everybody must want these things done in different ways and with different strengths".

I was still on my front, my arse facing Matt was up on his knees. He gently massaged my hole with his hand.

"Is this okay?" He asked.

I gently nodded in reply, burying my head into the pillow. I heard and felt him move around on the bed, and a moment later his fingers were massaging my hole again, but this time covered in lube.

I moaned gently.

His left hand reached out to hold mine which was held by my side, while his right hand got my hole wetter and wetter. One of the side effects of Matt's hesitancy to be too fast or rough with his hands and fingers was that he was teasing me. My cock was hanging below my hole so that it was erect between my legs.

"You're dripping!" Matt said.

"Of course I fucking am," I gasped with pleasure. "Do you know how much you're teasing me?"

"Am I?" he asked innocently.

"Yes, it's fucking agon..."

Before I could end that sentence, he slipped two lubed fingers into my hole.

My moans could have been heard by the anonymous gentleman a few streets away had he happened to be in town.

It's quite difficult to tell you the sounds and noises of the next few minutes.

"Oh fuck. Matt. Yes," was essentially the best that I could muster in terms of words. Otherwise, I was reduced to moaning intensely and grabbing every bit of bedpost and fabric that would take my grip. Matt meanwhile enjoyed the squidgey, lubey and squelchey sounds of his fingers in my arsehole. He veered from two fingers to one and then back to two. He veered from fingering me fast to fingering me slow.

Finally, I veered from being on my front to being on my back.

"Would you like to fuck me?" I asked.

He nodded, with a hint of nervousness that emphasised his beauty. I got a condom and asked if he would like me to put it on for him. He nodded. I'm on PrEP but I would still feel more comfortable knowing he felt suitably protected. I put it over his cock, lubed him up - and lubed myself just a little bit more - and held my legs aloft.

"Just ease it in," I said. "If you feel uncomfortable or want to stop, we can".

He leant over me and kissed me. He then got back on his knees, held my leg with his left hand for balance while his cock eased close to my hole with his right hand. The tip gently penetrated the surface of my hole. He looked at me intently. I nodded and took a deep breath to coincide with his movements.

And then he was inside of me. He held my thighs with his hands and smiled at me.

"Hey" he said softly.

"Hey".

"Is this comfortable?"

I nodded, smiling. "It feels amazing".

Matt gently fucked me. His eyes went from open to closed as he concentrated on his efforts. Slowly in and out as my arse got used to his cock, as he got used to fucking me. I was quite sure that he had never done anal before.

"Does this make me a top?" Matt asked, smiling.

"Good knowledge! Or un activo in Spanish, if you prefer. But only a top *for now*."

"What do you mean?"

"You might become a little bottom boy bitch", I said as I wrapped my hand around his back and gently slapped his arse. "You never know".

Matt laughed, and this spurred him on to fuck me harder. Our moans intensified, with Matt continually looking down to make sure that I wasn't in pain. The reality was anything but. Matt was getting into this. He pounded me harder and his hands gripped over my thighs.

"It seems you quite enjoy being the little bottom boy bitch," Matt grinned at me.

I laughed. "Just fuck me, alright?"

He bent in to kiss me, still fucking me. He was getting very sweaty, and his forehead was wet as it touched mine.

"Let's change up. Ease out". I said.

"Oh okay". Matt eased out. His cock was still rock hard.

"Lie down".

I climbed on top of him and kissed him, and worked my arse down onto his cock.

"Oh wow... fuck, fair play," said Matt, enjoying the new sensation. There was no need to ease in gently now. I was straddling Matt, and we were both fucking horny. I started riding him quickly, bouncing on his cock. We made that wonderful slapping sound as my arse landed on his thighs. My hands grasped his stomach for support. I slowed down for a breather.

"How does it feel?" He asked.

"It hits my insides and I can feel you in me. I love it."

"It doesn't hurt?"

"Not now. It did when I first did it".

"Now it doesn't hurt you at all?"

"No, not really"

"Oh okay, great".

He took this as his cue to thrust his cock right in me and thrusted hard. He pounded my arse like a caged animal released from his captivity. I fell forward due to the pressure he was powering into me. He lifted his arse a bit to improve the angle while my arms wrapped around his head.

"Yes. Fuck me". I moaned, quite involuntarily.

I may have mentioned this to you before - many times, probably - but I am a raging slut. I can take a cock in my arse. And Matt's cock is not huge. But... he was fucking pounding me and I was fucking loving it. My cock was twitching.

"I'm getting close," said Matt.

"Oh fuck yes. Fuck me."

I started to wank my cock but it didn't need much jerking. I had been holding in my load for a few minutes. Matt pushed my hand away and grabbed my cock. He started wanking it hard.

"Oh fuck," I cried. "Yes Matt. I'm gonna come."

My first shot hit his neck. My second landed on his chest. My third back to his neck. Then it shot and it shot and it shot over his stomach.

"Oh my god. Wow", Matt gasped.

"Don't you dare stop fucking me. Fuck me", I begged of him.

Matt pounded me. His moans intensified and his eyes closed as he got closer and closer.

"I'm gonna come mate. Mate, oh mate. Fuck".

He pounded me one last time and held his cock deep in my arse. I couldn't feel his load - the joys of safer sex - but I could feel the pressure sinking away from his body. I gently eased my hole away from his cock.

"This, mate, is the classiest part of the evening".

I slowly removed his condom and held it in my left hand while my right hand reached for a hand towel to clean my load off his body. I tied the condom up and put it in the bathroom bin.

I came back and Matt hadn't moved. He was breathing heavily and slowly getting the energy back to speak.

"Wow. That was hot mate".

I sat down next to him and held his hand.

"It was. How do you feel?"

"Good! I mean, exhausted. But fuck. I never thought I'd do that. I'm glad I did."

I leant down and kissed him.

"Shower?"

Matt nodded. We had a quick shower and then we were ready for bed. I put my underwear on. Matt stayed naked.

It was my turn to be the little spoon. Matt held my stomach with his right arm. He kissed my back.

"I quite enjoyed you shooting all over me" Matt said, unprompted.

I smiled. "Imagine how I felt with you shooting *in* me".

We fell asleep quickly.

Chapter Twenty Three

I woke up and it was hammering down with rain. I checked my watch and it was 6:30am. A wet Monday morning. And a working day.

Again, Matt was already awake before me. I heard the shower running.

He was quite quiet in the shower. No singing, no whistling, no humming. Not like me. My morning serenading screeches could be heard by Mrs Barnstable in Flat 2.

Matt came out a few minutes later, in his underwear. Fucking beautiful man.

"Morning!" he said, cheerily.

I smiled sleepily. "Hey. It's fucking Monday".

"It certainly is mate. How's your day looking?"

"I'm in virtual meetings all day. I've got a sales pitch presentation so I'll actually have to wear a shirt."

"But naked from the waist down, right?"

I laughed. "Sure. How about you?"

"Mondays are busy delivery days. I'll head home, pick up the van then straight off to the depot."

He walked over and kissed me on the forehead.

"Last night was incredible mate."

"Yeah. It was."

He started to get dressed.

"I need to rush. Hope you don't mind."

"God no, crack on. I need to do the same."

"I'll text you later".

Matt headed off and I sleepily got my day going. Shower, clothes, breakfast. Into the corner of my living room for another working day from home.

Last night really was incredible. Matt had felt comfortable to hang out, make out and eat my arse out, then pound me to my hole's content. He had also stayed over. A few times now. And hugged me and kissed me. And had breakfast with me. And smiled at me. My fuckbuddies didn't do that.

I didn't really know how to feel about Matt. If it was somebody else, it would be pretty easy: they would either drift off to being a passive friend who occasionally fucked me, or they would become a boyfriend.

I still didn't expect Matt to become my boyfriend. He could easily become a fuck buddy, or he could easily drift away and decide that this life isn't for him. Not many drifters give me a morning kiss on the forehead though.

My presentation went well. I may have made a new potential client. My boss remarked that I was particularly cheerful.

Matt texted me that evening.

"Hey mate! Thanks for last night. How do you feel about a beer this week? Thursday?X"

"Thank you! It was great. Thursday sounds great. See you then x"

Chapter Twenty Four

I had a pretty nice week. I went to the gym a couple of times and I was definitely in a good patch of training. I was starting to feel properly fit again for the first time since gyms had reopened after covid. I was even getting an eye or two from some of the fitter guys in the gym.

I hadn't hooked up with anybody else lately. Although I've got a high sex drive, if I have a really good fuck I don't need anything else for a while. Nevertheless, as I headed out to the city centre on Thursday night to meet Matt, I still browsed the apps. As much out of habit as anything else.

I like the gay apps on Thursday nights. Lots of new guys appear in the grid as they visit for the weekend. Even better, they stay in city centre hotels. Fit gays, discreet gays, discreet straights. You name it, they're around.

I exchanged messages with a few of the guys. "Hey, welcome". "Hey, hot pics. Where are you staying?" Etc. Etc.

Matt wandered in. He was wearing a casual pink shirt and a tight pair of jeans with trainers. In this friendly old man pub, he stood out like a fucking sexy sore thumb.

I stood up and we had a warm embrace.

"I don't know what I prefer: your cock or your hugs".

Matt laughed. "In this place, let's go with hugs! Pint?"

I nodded and a couple of minutes later, Matt brought a couple of pints to our table.

"How was your week?" I asked.

"Yeah really good mate thanks. I had a house move this week. They're starting to get back into full swing now so I'm winding down some of the delivery days a bit as house moves pay better. She was a really sweet old lady and tipped well so that was great."

"That's really sweet. Do you work alone or do you have a team?"

"There's another guy who does deliveries part time who appreciates the work. If it keeps getting busier, then I might look to hire him full time".

"That's great."

We discussed a bit more about his work and my work. He also asked about my family.

"Do they live here?"

"No, I moved here for university then stayed. They live further north towards Glasgow. I go and see them once a month or so."

"I've got a house move to Glasgow soon. I could probably drive you there if timings work out. I could definitely drive you back anyway as the van will be empty".

"Ah. That could work well! Thanks."

"Would your parents welcome me in for a cuppa?"

"You mean you'd use their bathroom then pound their arses?" I smiled.

Matt nearly spat out his beer. "Hahaha. Something like that. Do your parents know about your slutty behaviour?"

"They know that I'm pretty chilled about this sort of stuff. They make an effort to support me, like they marched at pride with me before covid, and they've stopped asking me about when I'm going to get a boyfriend. They respect that I do things a bit differently".

"But you're not totally closed to a boyfriend, right?"

"Not totally closed. But I just know that I like that freedom. Take this," I said, pointing to me and him, "it's been so great having you spontaneously come into my life. That probably wouldn't have happened even if I had been in an open relationship".

"I understand that. These last couple of weeks, I can definitely see where you're coming from. It was really nice to stop worrying about the consequences of things and just enjoy finding them with you."

"It's been so nice to see you relax and enjoy yourself. Do you know what might come next for you?"

"What do you mean?"

"Like, do you want to keep hanging out and we can discuss how we feel about this? Or do you want to explore other things with men? Do you want to start seeing girls again?"

"Good questions..." Matt laughed as he answered. "I don't know. What do you think I should do?"

It was my turn to laugh.

"Well... obviously whatever you want. I don't see why you can't consider all three! At least contemplate them. It seems you that enjoy pounding my arse..."

Matt nodded, smiling.

"So that's number one." I continued. "You might enjoy getting back out and going on a date or starting one or two profiles online. That's number two. And who knows, you might enjoy checking out the apps yourself or meeting another guy. I'm not the only bitch bottom slut in the world."

We smiled at each other.

"I don't know. That last one - meeting other guys - feels unlikely for now. I've enjoyed playing around and exploring with you precisely because it's you. I don't mean this rudely mate - the opposite, if anything - but I don't think that my attraction to you is just physical. You've stirred something up in me that I don't think other guys would. But I might be wrong. Who knows."

"But you might enjoy dating or thinking about dating again?" I asked.

"Maybe. Or even just having some fun. I've probably earned it".

"You definitely have".

"I don't really know what that looks like. I don't know how to flirt or how to get out there".

"You don't realise how hot you are, do you?" I asked.

He laughed. "Even if that's right, that doesn't make it easy to actually meet or strike up a conversation with someone"

"That's true. That's where online is useful to be fair".

"Yeah".

A barmaid came over to collect some empty glasses at the next table. She was probably around our age, slim and in great shape. She wore black jeans and had a cool overshirt hanging over a t-shirt.

She smiled at us but particularly smiled at Matt. He smiled back, innocently. She walked back to the bar.

"It's my round, but I reckon she might enjoy you going to the bar".

"What? Don't be daft - she's just being polite".

"Maybe. Only one way to find out". I smiled and gave him my card to get the beers. But he refused.

"Alright, alright. Same again?"

I went to the bar and got two more beers. I had a friendly chat with her.

"You guys are a bit younger than our regular crowd here," she said.

"Yeah, we're old men at heart".

She smiled. "Are you guys just mates or a couple?"

"We're good mates. Why do you ask?"

"No reason - testing my gaydar a bit. I thought you guys might be a cute couple".

"Ha. Well thanks. I'm gay so you're half-right".

"And him?"

"He's... just a very sweet guy".

"How intriguing." She smiled and went to serve another customer. I took the beers back to our table.

"Thanks. How was she?" Matt asked.

"She's great. Although I've no idea if she's into you, into both of us or a lesbian. Maybe all three".

"I can relate to that". We laughed and clinked glasses.

After a pause, Matt asked. "How would you feel if I went on a date with a girl or had fun with other people?"

"I would be fine. I don't think I would be jealous of anything you might end up doing. I am building some strong feelings for you, but they're not more than a warm friendship. I think…", I laughed as I stuttered through my answer. "If you end up fooling around with others and enjoying it, or you end up going on dates and something more conventional follows for you, then as long as you feel happy and comfortable about it then I'll be rooting for you".

"And if I'm enjoying spending more time with you and doing those things with you?"

"Then I'll be smiling about it and rooting for your cock in my hole".

We laughed and clinked glasses again. I looked over to the bar and noticed that the barmaid was still looking and smiling in our direction.

Matt had noticed too.

"Did you tell her anything about us?"

"Not really, although she did ask. I told her I was gay, and that you were a sweet guy."

"What did she say?"

"She smiled and said she was intrigued".

Matt glanced her way and smiled.

We stayed for another pint and just enjoyed the rest of the night. As we left the pub, we waved and said goodbye to the barmaid.

"I should just head home tonight. I have an early start tomorrow for another move", Matt said.

"Same", I replied. "This has been really good fun".

"It has! I'll drop you a text with dates for my Glasgow trip," Matt suggested.

We walked home until our paths parted and we ended with the customary hug. I didn't bother checking the apps. It was a nice night to let my horn build up and shoot a big load another day.

Chapter Twenty Five

Matt sent me through the details for his work van trip to Glasgow and confirmed that he would gladly have me for company if I wanted to visit my parents. It would be nice to get out of the flat, have a few days off work and go visit them. And a long trip with Matt would be fun.

That was a little while away though and first, it was the weekend. I got together with a few friends on Saturday night. We had a nice meal at my friend's home, a bottle of wine in one of the classier(ish) gay bars followed by a boogie in one of the trashier ones.

I fucking love my friends. Like me, they had lived alone or without loved ones during the pandemic and like me, they had found it fucking miserable. We had stayed as sane as we could with video calls and online board games and chatter about how much we missed cock, but nothing matched the fun we would have just being out for a night.

A small part of the evening had been spent discussing Matt. They had all met him the night that he had defended us from his homophobic friend.

They asked how we knew each other. They joked about the straight man piss fetish that I might be developing. They asked if we had done anything else. I firmly denied. I saw no benefit in muddying the waters.

We got another drink and had a good dance. As the night wore on, I was quite happily drunk and having a wonderful time.

I got a tap on the shoulder. I turned around, and it took me a moment to recognise who it was.

It was the barmaid.

"Oh hi!"

"Hey. I'm Claire."

We moved to a slightly quieter space.

"Hey, I'm Tom. When you asked me if we were gay. I never thought to return the question!"

She smiled. "I'm bi. Pan. Open minded and relaxed."

I smiled in return and we had a warm hug.

"Is your mate not here?" She asked.

"No he's not. I'm just with my friends tonight."

"Pity". She smiled.

"I'll tell him you said that!"

"Do. Although it's great to see you too".

"Ah. The afterthought. I'm flattered". She laughed, and she meant well. Sort of. "I should get back to my pals," she said. "Maybe see you again, Tom".

"Yeah. You too". We hugged again. She kissed me on the cheek.

I got back to my mates, although one of them had joined some other friends elsewhere and gone off to the sauna. The rest of us stayed for one more then went our separate ways.

I got into bed and checked my phone. A text from Matt.

"Hey mate! Hope you had a great night. I had a pint with my mates tonight too. My mate - unprompted - was super apologetic about his behaviour to you guys the other week. His girlfriend has even made him watch It's A Sin. #babysteps X"

My heart swelled almost as much as my cock at reading that.

Chapter Twenty Six

Sunday morning came around and with it a hangover. Nothing that some fresh air and a swim wouldn't solve.

I responded to Matt's text from last night.

"Hey! That's so great. It's A Sin is a wonderful programme and he'll learn a lot. Did you have a good night?"

"Yeah! Really good. How was yours?"

"It was so nice. We had a great night. I ran into that barmaid that we saw the other night in one of the bars! She's called Claire and she's bi/pan".

"Tbh, I'm not sure what pansexual means..." Matt replied.

"Basically that she doesn't really think about sex and gender when thinking about who she finds attractive."

"Ah okay. That's cool."

"She pretty clearly thinks you're hot..."

"She's got eyes? ;)"

"Hahaha. Cocky".

"Haha. She doesn't know about us though? I don't... mind. I guess I'm just enjoying the privacy."

"Oh yeah don't worry. I just told her I'm gay, you're friendly etc etc".

"She was kinda hot..."

"Yeah, I can see what you mean. She looked pretty hot last night in her party gear last night."

"You mean you would let her rim you?" He asked.

"I would let Mrs Barnstable from Flat 2 rim me if she was good at it," I replied.

A few more texts and laughing emojis followed and we made plans to see each other that night. I headed out for a swim. Winter was starting to bite and it was getting very cold. I kept an eye out in the pool and sauna for any straight married man who might want me to swallow his load, but nothing doing today.

I got home and had a relaxing evening. It was quite late when Matt buzzed my flat.

"Hey, it's me," he said.

"Come on up," I replied.

He came in and gave me a hug.

"Sorry I'm a bit late. I've not long finished deliveries."

It was 10:30pm.

"Oh shit. That's late".

"Yeah... Some days you just get a lot of the same day or next day delivery orders and you get decent rates if you do them. Especially on a Sunday."

"Fair enough. Well, hey. Make yourself comfy."

"Thanks. And... Do you fancy coming with me to Glasgow?"

"Yeah, if you don't mind the company?" I asked.

"Mind? I'd love it!"

"Okay awesome. I might go up a few days earlier to spend some time with my parents then come back with you".

"Sounds good".

"Will you get some sleep? It's like an eight hour drive?"

"Yeah, I'll get a hotel somewhere"

"You could stay with us? We have a spare bed. My parents won't mind"

"They don't need to do that."

"They love having guests! They're retired and bored. Obviously if you'd rather a hotel go for it, but please it would save you some money and it'd be nice"

"Okay great! Do I get to see photos of baby Tom?"

"Oh my mum will insist on it."

Matt smiled. "Can we go to bed?"

I nodded.

We got ourselves ready and started to undress down to underwear.

"Fuck it's cold in here!" Matt said, shivering and laughing.

"It's definitely snuggling weather!"

We got into bed, me in some white trunks and Matt in sporty blue boxers. We were both shivering and cold and hugged each other to keep warm.

"Hey," Matt said sweetly. He kissed me gently on the lips. "I'll be honest mate, I've been looking forward to this all day. There's just something about it".

I knew what he meant. It was very nicely relaxed. I turned off the light, and we both fell asleep quite quickly. Matt assumed the big spoon role once more, although we changed up a few times during the night as the bed warmed up and us with it. I woke up in a bit of a daze quite early - just after six - and it was still dark outside. One of those mornings where it was so fucking cold outside of the bed and so fucking cosy inside of it.

But I was the only one under the duvet. Matt was putting his trainers on. He walked over and gave me a kiss on the forehead.

"Morning mate."

"Morning", I sleepily replied. "You're up early. I can make some breakfast if you like?"

"No, it's okay. Thanks mate. I'm gonna get home, do a few things then head off in the van. I didn't wanna wake you. You looked so peaceful!"

"Haha, I don't feel peaceful. I've got a hard-on and sleep in my eye".

Matt felt my crotch through the duvet and quickly found out that I was telling the truth.

"You do! Oh wow".

Matt sat on the bed and placed his hand under the duvet. His hand touched my thigh. I screamed.

"Fuck, your hand is cold!"

He laughed. "Sorry! It's fucking chilly this morning. Now quit whining."

His hand massaged my cock through my boxers. He kissed me, and while his left hand stroked my hair, his right hand was rubbing my dick. He ripped off the duvet and pulled my pants down. It was fucking cold but it felt amazing.

I moaned while I closed my eyes once more. Matt got on his knees between my legs. His right hand slowly wanked my cock while his left hand stroked my thigh and balls.

He gently kissed my legs then slowly moved his mouth to my cock. He kissed my dick softly. Matt had never sucked my cock or even come close to putting my cock in his mouth before.

"I hope this is obvious, but you really don't have to do anything you don't want to," I reassured him.

Matt smiled. He kissed my cock again. He gently licked it with his tongue. I moaned. He then spat on it, and wanked it slowly.

"Fuck. This is a nice way to wake up," I said.

He spat on it again. Combined with my pre-cum, my cock was now making that noise. You know the noise: squidgy. It's not the most romantic sound. But hey, it feels fucking good right?

I sometimes had to pinch myself in moments like this. I had just enjoyed a spoon with a gorgeous, friendly and intelligent guy who was now between my legs, wanking my cock because firstly, he wanted to and secondly, he knew how much I wanted him to.

He spat on his left hand and spread his fingers over my hole. He gently teased my arse while he sped up his motion with his right hand. I suddenly realised I hadn't shot a load in quite a while.

"Fuck. Matt, I'm close."

"Yeah. Your cock is dripping!"

"Fuck. Oh mate. Matt. Matt. I'm gonna cum."

My moans increased as Matt maintained his speed. I shot. Everywhere. The first shot was over my head and hit the bedpost.

"Wow. Morning mate!" Matt was openly giggling at me while draining me of my load. The second shot hit my chin. The third hit my cheek. The fourth hit my chest. My body was jolting and I was gasping for air.

Matt's hands never moved from my cock and arse, and his eyes never moved from watching my load shoot everywhere. Gradually, I calmed and returned to the room. Matt grabbed a hand towel. He wiped his hands, and then laughed as he wiped my head board. He threw the towel to the floor.

"Now I definitely need to run. Thanks for having me over. See you soon?"

"Yes please".

Matt leaned in and kissed me.

"Have a good day buddy." Matt left my bedroom and a moment later I heard the front door close.

Chapter Twenty Seven

Later that day I got a text from Matt. He wondered if I enjoyed the wake up call. He told me how horny he had felt in the van all day. I insisted that if he was going to insist on waking me up like that, he should stay every night. We agreed to meet for a pint that night.

During the day, I rang my parents. As expected, they were thrilled that I would be visiting for a few days and more than happy to host Matt too.

My mum gently enquired as to whether the spare bed should be made up too or just my old double bed. I said that the spare bed would be good. Matt was clearly becoming more comfortable with me but that didn't necessarily mean he was comfortable being that open with everybody. Least of all my mother.

I got to the pub before Matt and found that Claire was working again.

"Oh hey. Nice to see you".

"Welcome back. What can I get you?"

I chose one of the local beers.

"Are you meeting your friend again?" she asked.

"I am indeed".

She smiled at this news, and gave me my pint.

"Thanks! Chat to you in a bit".

Matt arrived a couple of minutes later. I saw him have a very similar interaction with Claire to the one that I had just had.

"Hey!" he gave me a hug. "I see she's here again".

"Hey!" I smiled. "Yeah".

"I've been thinking about this, you know".

"What, Claire?"

"Yeah. Well, anybody really. I don't mind anybody knowing that we're close like this. At least, I don't mind people knowing that I'm close with a guy. I don't want to broadcast every bit of information, but I don't mind people knowing that".

"Good. Because I've already told her that you wanked me off this morning and my cum hit the headboard".

Matt laughed.

"She seems the sort that might enjoy knowing that mate, to be fair. But I mean that if people ask about us, I know we're not a couple or anything. But if people make it awkward by asking questions about me, I don't mind if people put two and two together. If somebody cottons on that I've done a gay thing with a gay guy, it's fine with me".

"Okay. Well, thank you. I don't think anyone is making it awkward, but it is great how comfortable you feel about this."

We smiled and enjoyed a drink. It was quite quiet in the pub. Claire was on her phone at the bar. There was another bar colleague too. There were almost as many staff as there were customers.

"If anybody was likely to be interested in what we get up to, it might be her", I said.

"Yeah. She's part of the reason I said it. She was asking about us and how she had seen you in the gay bar at the weekend. I think she likes us".

"I think she likes you. How do you feel about that?" I asked.

"I don't really know to be honest. I mean, I don't know her. How do you feel about that?" He asked me in return.

"It kinda turns me on. It kinda makes me feel a tiny bit jealous. Which kinda turns me on a bit more".

Matt smiled. "Would you do anything with her?" He asked.

"Me?" I replied. "Probably not. I'd watch you fuck her".

Matt laughed. "You're not serious?"

"I would genuinely love that. But no, I'm not being serious. Although, if I wanked to it, I'm pretty sure my load would hit the headboard".

Matt laughed. Claire came to our table.

"Hey guys. Can I get you another beer?"

"I'm off to London in the morning, so I'll regret this. But yes please! Same again," Matt replied.

She smiled, collected our empty glasses and walked away.

"How do you feel, chatting like this?" I asked. "In a few weeks, you've gone from having one woman in your life, to rimming me, fucking me, spooning me, wanking me off the morning after spooning me, then going for a pint with me while I tell you how much I'd love to watch you fuck a stranger".

Matt smiled while supping his pint. "I mean, when you put it like that... I don't really know how I feel. Part of me is waiting for it to fall apart and just get overwhelmed by it all. But for now I'm feeling good. And I did all of those things because I wanted to, not because I wanted to fuck anybody who opened their door to me".

At that precise moment, Claire returned with the card machine and two pints, looking amused and bemused in equal measure. I started to laugh. Matt looked embarrassed.

"Hi! Sorry," he said. "We were just..."

"Discussing who you're fucking?" Claire asked with a grin.

She smiled at both of us, put the beers on the table and walked away. We both laughed.

"I think that means you *have* to fuck her now," I said. Matt jokingly put his head in his hands. I could see Claire was still laughing as she walked back to the bar.

"Have you ever had a threesome?" Matt asked, trying to regain his composure.

"Yes, with men: each time with couples where I was the third guy. I don't mind it but it's not really my thing. I prefer one on one. I don't really need to ask if you've had a threesome?"

"Nope. I've had sex with two people in my whole life. Emma and you."

"Does it interest you?"

"Not really. It all has a bit too much going on."

We chatted some more, drifting from discussing men to women to beer to whatever else. Matt got us another pint. He was there for a couple of minutes with Claire, so I went to the bathroom. As I came back, Matt was back with a couple of pints at the table.

"Well?" I smiled and asked.

"She gave me her number. She asked me what my deal was."

"What did you say?"

"I said I had no idea! But she seemed cool and suggested that maybe we might hang out sometime. The three of us".

"The three of us? I don't think I need to be there," I replied.

At that moment, Claire came over to our table, with a pint and a whisky chaser.

"Hey. My boss says I can finish early as it's so quiet. Do you mind if I join you for a drink?"

"Sure". We both smiled and made room. She downed the whisky in one. We looked a bit surprised and a bit impressed at the same time.

"Who exactly were you discussing fucking earlier?" She asked, without hesitation.

Matt put his head into his hands with embarrassment once more.

"Nobody!" Matt replied. "Tom is relaxed about these things. I'm not".

"He means I'm a bit more of a slut than he is". I translated.

"A bit?" Matt interjected.

Claire smiled. "So you're bi?"

"No idea. Maybe," Matt replied.

"And you?" Claire asked, looking in my direction.

"I'm gay. Albeit an open-minded one".

"Okay. Well this is interesting! Drinks?"

Claire went and got us another pint and a whisky each.

"I knew there was something about you guys when I met you," she said. "Something different. I liked it."

"Are you single?" I asked.

"Yeah," Claire replied. "Bar work isn't great for a romantic life. Tinder and apps help me meet people but I'm happy being single for now".

"And where do you sit sexually"? Matt asked.

"Where do I sit?" She replied. "I mean usually..."

"No!" Matt interrupted before the filthy answer came. "Fuck my life. I mean... sorry... are you more cautious like me or more relaxed like him?"

"I'm more like him", she replied, pointing in my direction.

"Okay. That's probably for the best". Matt replied. We all laughed and had a sip of whisky.

The evening progressed and Claire quite quickly caught us up with more beer and whisky. I was feeling quite nicely drunk and I'm sure Matt was the same.

Nice and interesting all this was, I wasn't sure how I wanted this evening to progress. I was definitely intrigued. Claire was as relaxed and open-minded as me, albeit more assertive than me. And she was hot. Part of me was curious at the idea of doing things with a woman. And I was very curious at helping Matt to explore his boundaries. I would be very relaxed about this if it was just my own curiosities and boundaries at stake.

But it wasn't just my own. Matt had done an awful lot in the space of a few weeks, but at no point had I had a sense that I was pushing him into a space where he was uncomfortable. Tonight, I wasn't sure. Would Matt enjoy doing anything with her? Would he enjoy me being there with him? Would he enjoy it because of me being there or in spite of me being there?

I looked at him. Matt looked excited and nervous in equal measure. I hadn't seen him like this. His hands were fidgeting with nervous energy. I felt like he was trying to push himself through this. Like he was fighting himself, his reservations and his insecurities.

I didn't know what my role was in this scenario: whether to support him by agreeing with every question and action, encouraging his exploration, or whether I should support him by encouraging caution.

As I was pondering all of these questions, Matt and Claire were drinking more and talking more. Claire was beginning to ask more and more personal questions about his sexual attractions and preferences. Matt was answering with hints of caution, but also throwing that caution to the wind by asking questions in return.

"Where are you guys going after this?" Claire asked.

"Home, I hope! It's a school night", I replied.

"Yeah," Matt sighed. "We could have a nightcap at yours?" He looked at me as he asked.

"Erm... yeah okay. We could," I replied.

"I'm game", Claire said.

"We don't have to," Matt said quietly in my direction.

"No," I said. "I'm good with that".

"OK", Matt said. He tapped his hands with a sense of purpose on the table, as if he was geeing himself up for what might be about to happen.

Chapter Twenty Eight

We got a taxi back to my flat.

We made our way upstairs to the top floor. I led, Claire in the middle and Matt last of all. Claire affectionately touched my hand as we walked upstairs. Thankfully, I had turned the heating on in advance so that it would not be ice cold when we got back.

"I might need another whisky," Matt said, heading to the cupboard.

Claire nodded in approval at the suggestion. She walked over to Matt and kissed him. She was straight in with a tongue, and Matt was a bit caught off guard. He put his hands nervously on her waist. As she took a step back, she smiled at him.

"Erm... okay". Matt laughed and his voice shaked. "Whisky". He walked into the kitchen to get whisky and glasses.

I felt even more unsure and nervous about this than I had in the pub. Part of me felt exhilarated at the prospect of trying something new, and especially so that I was trying something new with Matt. And he had instigated this more than me, although maybe not as much as Claire. I remained completely unsure of what my role was in this situation.

As Matt returned, I tried to offer something useful that might at least set the tone for what was about to follow.

"I guess we should cover some ground rules", I said. If anybody is uncomfortable with anything at any point, just say. Or even just don't say and feel free to stop. Does that sound okay?"

Matt nodded, even though his face was conveying anything other than confidence and affirmation.

"Agreed", Claire replied. She waved her glass in our direction and drank some more whisky.

Claire walked up to me and kissed me. Again, no messing around. I immediately got a nice taste of whisky. It was pretty hot. But so, so different. I went to hold her head and felt more hair - and softer hair - than I had ever felt before.

"Is that the first time you've kissed a girl?" She asked.

"It's probably the first time I've enjoyed it". Me and Claire both smiled and kissed again. Matt sat on a chair and just watched as he took his trainers off, hopefully enjoying what he was watching.

"Have you done anything with girls?" She asked.

"Years ago. One sucked me off. That was it. I prefer giving pleasure..."

Before I could continue, Matt spluttered as he sipped his whisky. "I can vouch for that. He fucking loves it". We all started laughing.

"Can I see?" Claire asked.

I walked over to Matt, and he stood up. I kissed him, and I quickly felt more relaxed. He seems to physically calm and settle into my arms. Kissing him was now becoming more than just a wonderful thrill, but a comforting and welcoming sensation too.

I moved to my knees and undid his belt buckle, then the button and fly of his jeans. I gently pulled them down and his underwear with them. He was sporting a semi. His cock really was just beautiful. Nicely meaty. Nicely veiny. A head that pulled back but not too far. Pretty much straight but with just a hint of a bend. It throbbed. It pulsed. It was just a joy.

He was already leaking a bit of pre-cum. I licked it with my tongue while my hands caressed his thighs. Claire stood and watched, sipping her whisky with one hand and the other resting on her crotch.

I slowly took his cock in my mouth. Matt groaned and grabbed my hair with his right hand. His whisky still sat tightly in his left.

Claire undid her trousers and took them off. She took her top off too. She had a dark grey bra and matching pants on. She sat down and enjoyed her whisky while her other hand drifted around her body.

Matt wasn't sure where to look. He went from looking down at my mouth, to closing his eyes, to looking at Claire. She smiled at him. He nervously smiled back and looked away again.

Matt was still semi-hard. His cock occasionally throbbed and jolted, but he wasn't yet fully erect. I looked towards Claire as she undid her bra. She had a great body. She teased her nipples with her fingers while her hands caressed her breasts. My eyes drifted lower though. Her hand was starting to feel inside her pants. I could tell that she was already wet.

I moved my mouth away from Matt's cock. I looked up at him and he nodded in a manner to suggest he was comfortable with me going over to her. I moved over without standing up so that I was still on my knees but now between Claire's legs. Matt removed his pants properly, and sat next to Claire on the sofa, looking beautiful but still a little uncomfortable. He removed his t-shirt and sat fully naked, stroking his cock. He was going soft again.

My hands worked their way up and down Claire's legs. She leaned back on the sofa and continued to run her fingers under her pants and over her pussy. Even though I had never done so to a woman before, I wanted to please Claire. I wanted to taste her.

I could see that just this sensation of my hands on her legs was enjoyable for Claire. Her pussy was clearly wet and her body was warm to touch.

I moved down to her ankles and kissed her calves. My hands massaged them and worked up her legs again, this time moving to the inside of her thighs. I pulled her pants down and removed them, looking up to see her pussy. It was completely hairless, a classic peach.

I was about to eat pussy for the first time, and it dawned on me that I was acting solely on instinct. Rewatching that famous scene from *Bound* in my mind wasn't going to help me out much in that moment. I would simply proceed with caution, and try to respond to what her body was telling me.

I gently moved towards her with my mouth. My tongue slid between her lips and pushed them out as my tongue slipped in between. Its flavour was quite enchanting. A primal instinct arose in me: I wanted it. I heard myself moan softly and my tongue naturally moved up and down.

My whole mouth started to work. My tongue worked, and then my lips, and then I found myself gently sucking her lips, before my tongue swirled around her swelling pussy. Claire's hand reached my head and I could feel her breathing in and out by the way she grabbed me. My hands continued to massage her thighs. They jolted every few seconds as my mouth explored her.

I moved her thighs wider and moved my mouth deeper. Her breathing became quite laboured, and her moans became heavier. She started to feel comfortable with my mouth around her pussy. She started to feel that she could direct me. She started to have confidence that my mouth would respond. When my tongue seemed to do the right thing, she pushed me in firmer, with a gentle whisper that affirmed my movements. My mouth was now firmly locked on her pussy.

"Fuck," was all that she managed to sigh.

I laughed all while my tongue continued to do its work. Matt stayed where he was on the sofa. Claire's hand moved from my head and moved over to grab his cock. Matt sighed, his cock still pretty soft. My own right hand moved from Claire's left thigh over to Matt's right thigh, caressing him gently.

Claire kissed Matt again, moving her hand back to my head to keep me where I was. She was getting very wet. She sat back on the sofa and suddenly both her hands were tightly gripping the back of my head. Each time she moaned, my head moved in just that little bit more.

Then ever so suddenly I found myself on familiar oral ground. She started to shake, she started to moan and groan more than previously. She started to thrust on my mouth. She started to tense a little more. She writhed around on the sofa. I did my best to match her involuntary movements as she got wetter and wetter onto my tongue.

"Can we stop?" Matt said.

"I'm sorry. I'm really sorry. Can we just. Can we just stop". Matt said again.

Chapter Twenty Nine

"Are you okay?" Claire asked.

"I'm fine, I'm just... I don't want to do this. I'm sorry," Matt replied.

"Of course. Sorry Matt". I said.

Matt put his clothes back on, quite sheepishly but with a clarity that had been missing in the preceding hours. Claire also put her clothes back on, looking a bit bemused. I was already clothed, trying to look concerned but also reassuringly in Matt's direction.

"I should probably go," Claire said.

Me and Matt both gently nodded apologetically, and in a few seconds she had gathered her things and was out the door. She had left without giving us her number. I suspect she felt pissed off with both of us as we headed home.

Matt sat down, let out a huge sigh and started to cry. I rushed to his side and sat down with him.

"Matt, I'm so sorry. I didn't know whether I should follow your lead and be enthusiastic about this or whether I should have stopped it myself. I'm sorry," I said.

"Fuck, don't be sorry Tom. It's me. I'm just... this was too much and I should have said as much sooner. I'm an idiot."

"You are not an idiot".

"I just had the chance to have sex with a hot girl and with you, and I couldn't get a hard-on. And now I'm crying. I'm a fucking fool, Tom".

I put my arms around him. As I held him, I started to reflect on why I had gone ahead with this. It was partly a test of my own feelings, maybe a sense of wanting to help Matt explore his own feelings, maybe a fear that I cannot offer him everything he wants, and maybe a fear that Matt cannot offer me everything I want.

At once, I felt surprised and confused at what had just happened, relieved and happy that Matt had wanted to stay with me in this moment, and a mix of fear and desire as to what I felt for him in return.

Underpinning all of this was a vast amount of beer and whisky consumed by us both... on a school night as well.

Matt spoke first.

"I just didn't feel right. She's sweet but I don't like her like that. And I like you like that, but I'm still figuring out what that means".

"That is allowed, you know. It's okay".

"Yeah. I think I should go".

"You don't have to. You can stay".

"I know, but I'm a bit afraid of what I'm going to say to you. And even by saying that, I'm going too far. Fuck's sake".

He got up, and put his coat on. "Sorry Tom. Goodnight". I stood up, he hugged me, and as fast as Claire had just a few minutes earlier, was gone.

Chapter Thirty

I woke up early the next morning, following a night where I barely slept. I was hungover and miserable.

I texted Matt to wish him a safe trip to London and to hope that he was okay.

I wouldn't see him again until we were both in Glasgow in a few days. The last time I saw him he was crying on my sofa. The next time I would see him, he would be meeting my parents for the first time.

It was a fucking mess.

I had a rubbish day at work, and a night made worse by an ongoing hangover and still no reply from Matt. The next morning came and went, as did the night. Still nothing. The following day, I went out for a walk to clear my head but I don't know that it did me any good.

As I got home, I looked around my flat and saw that I had let it become a bit of a state. And then I looked in the mirror and wondered the same thing.

This was why I stayed single. This is why I fucked around. In any other time, if I was feeling down I would simply log on to the apps and fuck my troubles away.

I lived in a part of town not far from the main university. That meant lots of students. Contrary to the popular stereotypes and stories, that did not necessarily make it a gay man's dream. Sure, lots of gym guys lived nearby, but they were mostly straight. Even if I got lucky and one was gay and online, they tended not to be chatty. Monosyllabic messages from bored and horny men who want to share some dick pics but don't want to make any effort.

But still... occasionally they would help me fuck my troubles away.

In any other time, I would log on and look at the local world around me. A student would message me. He would say hey. I would ask how he was. He would simply say he was horny.

The student would write very little. But he would be toned. He would be passive and bored, and often boring. But he would be hung. And he would be utterly forgettable. But he would be available right now.

He would not accommodate, so I would ask him if he would like to come over. I would send him my address and wait. I loved these moments. The anticipation. The excitement that my hole would give me in that moment. The tingling knowledge that it would be getting pounded in just a few minutes. The slight danger of that spontaneous meeting with a stranger.

I would hear my doorbell ring. I would buzz him up. I would leave the door ajar. I would get naked and wait on the bed, on all fours. He would walk in, follow my calls to my bedroom. He would be pleasantly surprised at the view that awaited him.

I would hear him take his clothes off. I would sneak a quick peek. I would see his cock already hard and waiting. I would see his six pack. Within seconds, I would feel his cold hands on my arse. I would feel him grab lube and squirt it over my hole.

He would slip it straight in. No messing about. No teasing. If Matt did this, I would gently teach him the importance of the gentle build-up of seduction. But for such encounters like these, there was no need. He would be fit and horny. I would be... well at least one of those things.

I would beg him to pound me and he would duly oblige. Within a few thrusts, he would be deep inside me. Not far from being painful. But my slutty abilities would always click in and I would take it like a queen.

Within seconds, he would shoot in my arse. He would apologise, as much to himself as to me. I would tell him it was fine. I would beg him to stay and fuck me again. I would assure him that he could manage. I would tell him that his spunk would be the perfect lubricant for round two.

That would persuade him, and I would get on to my back. My legs would be over his shoulders as he would pound me again. This time, he would last longer. He would not care less whether he was causing me pain or pleasure. I would be hard, but he would not care. I would not care less if I never found his name.

I would beg him to fuck me harder, knowing that the sore arse that would follow would be worth it. He would pound me again and again, making my bed springs long for the pandemic days when I would do nothing more strenuous than a bored wank. He would get close to shooting. He would start to grunt and sweat as he would get closer and closer until he would shoot one more time in my hole.

I would shoot my load at the same time, but this man would not care. He would pull out, wipe and stand up. He would put his clothes back on. He would maybe say thank you. He would maybe say that he would see me again. We would both know that that was probably a lie. Then he would leave.

Such an encounter would be both exhilarating and underwhelming. Thrilling yet a chore. Yet at various moments in my life when I had felt a bit down, a bit low, or even just a bit tired and horny and in need of a fuck, those encounters would be there when I needed them.

I wondered in that moment if I needed such an encounter now.

I continued to look in the mirror and decided, despite the misery this chance encounter with Matt was currently bringing me, that I did not.

"I miss you," I texted him.

Chapter Thirty One

It's a fucking long way to Glasgow.

It was seven thirty in the morning, and I had just boarded the train. Much though I loved my family and some of the old school friends who still lived locally, I had come very close to cancelling the whole thing. Matt had still not contacted me since leaving my flat the other day.

I settled in my seat and sent Matt a message. I hoped he was okay, and that he was still coming to Glasgow, but that if he wasn't that I understood.

I drifted asleep as the train drifted further north.

Do you know Glasgow? It's a beautiful city. An enchanting mix of buildings, people and culture. Some of those buildings happen to house some of the best pubs in the world. It had significant deprivation and poverty too. My parents had grown up in poverty and both grafted their way out of it, with a bit of good and bad luck along the way.

We were a small but loving family. They cared hugely for me without interfering too much in my life. So long as I had a smile on my face, they were happy. And they didn't give a flying fuck if that smile came from a woman, a man or both at the same time.

Nonetheless, if Matt did indeed pop up in Glasgow they would pepper him with questions. They would ask about me, they would ask about his life, they would ask about Emma if Matt dared mention her. Last week, part of me had been looking forward to it. Now, I was dreading it.

I arrived in Glasgow. I had agreed that I would meet my parents at home. I headed to the bus stop when...

"Surprise!" A shrieking tiny woman cried.

Fuck's sake, Mam.

"Oh Tom! Oh sweetheart." She was crying. I hugged her tightly. She was a wonderful woman. Mad as a box of frogs sometimes, but wonderful. It was just the second time since the pandemic began that I had been home.

"Good to see you, son." My Dad shook my hand. He wasn't really the hugging sort.

Despite my reservations, what actually followed was a most fabulous time. We went for a drink, then dinner, then another few drinks in some of my favourite pubs. My parents were on top form. Although they were starting to get to an age where telling me about the thrills and spills of daytime telly was the peak of their conversation, when they were in the mood they were a hoot on a night out.

It was now around ten o'clock and we had all had quite a bit to drink.

"So tell me about Matt, who is he?" My mum asked.

"Ssshhh, Abigail," my Dad piped up.

"I'm only asking who he is!"

I laughed. "You can ask anything you want. Matt is just a friend. I met him a few months ago. He works as a delivery driver and occasionally a removals driver. He happens to be in Glasgow for a job. It worked out as a nice excuse to come up and see you guys and take a few days off to visit".

"Well that's wonderful. I cannot wait to meet him," she said,

"I suspect the same for him. He will want expect to see baby photos".

"Well who wouldn't of my baby boy!" She drunkenly pinched my cheek.

We had a couple more drinks and then took a taxi home. I still had not heard from Matt. He wasn't due in Glasgow for another day or so but still, we had not spoken a word since he had left my flat in tears a few nights previous.

We got home and my parents had made the bed up for me already and everything was toasty and warm. I checked across the landing, the spare room was already done up too ready for Matt to sleep in a couple of days.

I hoped that he was alright.

My mum came in to wish me a good night and I was quickly under the sheets in my old bedroom. I looked around as I often did when I came back. My first wank had been in this room. And my second. And my hundredth. I had never brought a boy back here. Friends, yes. Sleepovers, yes. But no illicit wanking sessions. No secret blowjobs. Just video games and cans of shandy.

I checked my phone. Nothing.

Chapter Thirty Two

I slept badly but woke up quite early. I checked my phone, and saw that Matt had still not contacted me. My nostrils were tingling at the smells of a Scottish breakfast from the kitchen.

If you have never had the opportunity to try it, you should. The famous part is the Lorne sausage. Imagine the breakfast burger patty from a certain famous burger chain, but a bit nicer.

I quickly showered and went downstairs. My Mam was at the stove, slaving away. My Dad was at the table with a cuppa and the Scottish Daily Mirror. This had been their life for thirty years or so. Not much had changed.

"Morning! How did you sleep sweetheart?" My Mam asked me.

"Oh fine", I lied.

"What do you have planned today?"

"I'm meeting Rosie". Rosie is an old friend from school. "She is dog sitting for a friend so we'll head up a hill somewhere, then maybe we could all just chill out tonight?"

"Wonderful, darling!" My mum is as enthusiastic hungover at 8am as she is pissed at 10pm. My Dad barely looked up from the newspaper.

I devoured my breakfast then headed out to see my friend Rosie. I won't bore you too much with the details. We discussed very little of relevance to my particular story. She was lovely and her temporarily acquired dog was lovely, but she was a friend with whom I discussed work and clean social things, not Matt.

But we had a great time, and the fresh air was wonderful for me, and by the time I got home I was ready for a late afternoon nap and a lazy night with my parents.

We had another lovely time together that evening. We watched a shit film while talking shit, and just lazily lay around. We had spent many occasions doing the same over webcams and phone calls during the pandemic, but so much nicer to actually be doing it in the same room.

I had still not heard from Matt. I hoped that he was taking a few days in London with a load of accompanying driving time to just get himself relaxed, to have time with some friends, and to not worry about everything.

I worried that he was overthinking, replaying and regretting. Regretting Clare. Regretting threesomes. Regretting me.

I admonished myself at my hypocrisy. Here was me having a go at Matt for overthinking while I was overthinking every fucking thing in my mind.

"What time is Matt coming tomorrow?" My Dad asked.

Good question, Dad.

"I'm not sure," I answered truthfully. "A lot will depend on when he gets the house move finished. Early evening, I expect".

I got into bed. I had still not heard from Matt. I had not shot a load in days either. I thought about having a wank while thinking about him, reliving my gloriously isolated teenage years spent shooting over every bit of my room.

I thought about checking online to have a late night rendezvous. But that didn't feel appropriate, either because of my parents or because of Matt.

My phone buzzed.

"Hey Tom," it read. "I'm so sorry for being silent. Honestly, I've been a bit all over the place but I'm fine now. I will be on my way to Glasgow tomorrow and I'll keep you posted when I come over to you. I can't wait to see you. Night xxx"

Me too mate. Fuck. Me too.

Chapter Thirty Three

I replied to Matt in the morning. "Hey, I'm sorry you've been struggling. And I'm so sorry if I've played a part in that. Come chill out and have a great time with us, then we can get home and relax".

I went out into town with my parents and we did a bit of shopping, had some lunch and a nice wander about the city. Then my mother wanted to get us home so she could make sure the house was absolutely spotless. I reassured her that he was a removals driver and was used to shit being everywhere, nevermind that her home was spotless, but she insisted.

We got home and when she realised that everything was as clean as clean can be, we sat down and had a cuppa. I heard Matt's van pull into the drive about an hour later. I went out to meet him and gave him a hug. He looked a little drained and tired.

"Tom, it's so good to see you". He squeezed me tightly.

Our embrace was interrupted by a very excited mother coming out to greet us.

"Matt! Hello! Nice to meet you. Please call me Abigail and this is Tom's father, Derek".

"Abigail, Derek" Matt shook both their hands. "It's great to meet you both. Thank you for having me. It saves me a long drive home without any sleep".

"Our pleasure! Now can I get you a drink or would you like a shower or anything?"

"A shower would be great".

"I'll take over from here, Mam. Follow me".

I took Matt upstairs. I showed him his room and shut the door. I gave him a proper hug. We gripped each other tightly.

"How are you doing?" I asked.

"Yeah, I'm okay. I think I've just had a bit of a panicky time. But I'm okay. I missed you a lot".

He smiled at me, and I smiled at him. The last time I had seen Matt, he had been in pain. And we had both been in pain since. And here we were now, smiling at each other. Pain-free.

He kissed me, with a wetter, messier and sloppier kiss than we had ever had before. Fuck, it was nice to feel him around me again. I was grinning like a Cheshire cat.

Matt looked around my room. He found some old textbooks on shelves, photo frames, old video games, and one or two books that caught his eye.

"Chavs! I read this years ago. I used to read Owen Jones all the time. I remembered it was the first time I thought about myself politically. I used to think politics was about other people, not me. Did you feel the same when you read it?"

"I mean, sure," I replied. "I mainly just had a huge crush on him! But then I read it and loved it. I feel old thinking about that now, it was so long ago. Lots of old memories here".

Matt smiled and headed off for a shower. Afterwards I grinned and kissed him again, fighting the urge not to run my hands through his wet and floppy hair, never mind in his other floppy parts.

My mother cooked us a delicious meal and as expected Matt was peppered with questions. How had he met their son, how did he cope with his sarcasm and rude humour, what did he do for a living, how was lockdown, who were his family and how was their lockdown.

She asked him if he was seeing anybody, and if he too was a fellow gay. Derek shushed her. Matt laughed.

"It's okay! Although I don't really know the answer to that. I guess I don't really know or care".

I smiled, and both my heart and my cock jolted at his answer.

"Well, that's lovely. I don't know if there is a letter in LGBTQ for that," my mother responded. My Dad looked embarrassed. I was proud of their openness to these things.

"Are you single?"

"Yes. I'm widowed. My wife died a couple of years ago".

"Oh. Matt, that's awful. I'm sorry."

"Thank you. She had a tumour. It was quick and reasonably peaceful. I'm doing okay now. To be fair, your son has been a wonderful help".

Would you look at that? I have been a wonderful help. My mum held my hand with pride.

"We have a wonderful son," she beamed.

And that was her cue. Out came the baby photos. For the next hour or at the dinner table, my mother took Matt on an emotional journey through the life and times of dear baby Tom, from birth to childhood to spotty puberty to spotty adulthood and finally to now.

"What happened to you?" Matt asked.

"What do you mean?" I innocently replied.

"You used to be adorable. Now look at you".

My parents laughed. Matt had become quite the sassy shit in recent weeks. I smiled at him.

Not long ago this guy was just some fit lad pissing in my toilet. Now he was here making my parents proud of me, doing the sorts of things a boyfriend would do.

And I loved it.

I managed to persuade my parents to leave Matt alone, and we went out for a pint nearby. Matt remarked on how nice my parents are, and I remarked on how nice he had been with them.

"How are you feeling? I don't know if you want to talk about anything?" I asked.

Matt sighed.

"Yeah. Tom, I'm sorry I've been quiet. This has all just been a lot. I think I got carried away with how easy I found being with you, that I thought everything we did would be easy. So when we met Claire, and it kinda started stepping up the gear, I leant into it. But that was stupid of me, and I led you both on and I just should have stopped".

"I don't think I've helped you much. I should have stepped in much sooner to calm it all down".

"You don't need to apologise mate! I think I thought that I was enjoying having fun so I should just keep on pushing. But that's not true. I was enjoying my time with you. You. Not Claire, not fun fun fun. You".

I looked down, feeling a sense of pride and embarrassment in equal measure.

"And then," he continued "I got nervous about feeling like that about you. And so I stayed quiet for a bit. But I'm going to stop being nervous about it. I like you, Tom. And I'm just going to lean into that".

"I like you too, Matt". We smiled.

We drank our beer quietly for a few seconds.

"Does this mean we're going out?" I asked.

Matt smiled.

"I don't know. Maybe?"

"Maybe," I agreed.

"I don't want to push it. I know you have things a lot more settled than me and I'm still figuring all of this out".

"I disagree," I replied. "I may have got myself settled in my sexuality and my day to day thoughts on things. But I don't think I've felt about anybody the way I have about you. And that makes me excited, and it makes me uncomfortable, even if you then hug me and I feel comfortable again. Our experiences are fluid, and I'm figuring this out too. And that's okay".

Matt smiled again. "You're right. We're both figuring this out".

We drank our beer again quietly.

"It was very cool that you discussed your sexuality with my Mam".

"Yeah. That surprised me as much as you! But it felt good".

"I think there might be a letter for you on the LGBTQ+ spectrum, by the way. Have you heard of demisexuality?"

Matt shook his head.

"The basic idea is that you experience sexual attraction only once you have an emotional bond with somebody. And for some that might be limited to only straight experiences or a gay experiences, or something else, but it doesn't have to be".

"Are you modestly suggesting that I'm developing an emotional bond for you?" Matt asked.

I smiled. "Maybe I'm sheepishly telling you that I've developed one for you".

Matt grinned at me. He leaned across the table and kissed me.

Chapter Thirty Four

My Dad picked us up and drove us home. We got ready for bed and it was getting pretty late. My Mam was still shepherding everybody around.

"Now Matt, I've had the heating on in your room so you shouldn't be too cold, and there's a glass of water by your bedside table. If you need anything..."

"Mam! He's a grown man".

She tutted at me and ruffled my hair.

"Thank you Abigail," Matt interjected. "For everything. You've been so sweet".

My parents left us and went to bed. I hugged him.

"I would love to spoon you but I think it saves us questions in the morning if we don't," I whispered.

Matt nodded. He kissed me gently.

"I agree. Goodnight mate. Thank you".

We went to our separate beds. I slept well, buoyed by seeing Matt and having a good night with him. I woke up in the middle of the night, needing a piss. I walked past my parents' bedroom. I could hear them both snoring away.

I thought about going to Matt's bed. It would be so fucking nice to cuddle him. But no. Be sensible, Tom. Another day or so and we could do it when we got home.

I got back to my bedroom. I lifted the covers and got the fright of my life.

"Jesus!"

It was Matt.

"Sorry!" he whispered. "I couldn't sleep and I just wanna hold you mate".

I got into bed. "You scared the shit out of me," whispering and laughing in equal measure.

I kissed him. "Matt, thank you for tonight."

"Thank you mate. Now turn over".

I obeyed his orders - what else is a man to do - and he held me close. He kissed my back. His body was wonderfully warm and the cold Scottish winter was kept at bay by his presence.

"Goodnight mate".

Chapter Thirty Five

It was 7am. Matt awoke me by kissing my forehead and leaving to go back to his own room.

A couple of hours later we both surfaced separately from our rooms and enjoyed a classic Glasgow breakfast to fill us up before our long drive home. Well, Matt's long drive... I would just be a grateful passenger. He was looking rough but sexy today. He hadn't shaved for a couple of his days and his stubble was long and scratchy. He had a grey hoodie and black shorts. It was fucking cold but I guess his van had good heating.

My Mum tried to force sandwiches upon us but we insisted we would stop off on the way. Following some warm embraces and goodbyes, we were on our way. It was a clear day and the traffic looked good. We were just past halfway when Matt suggested we stop off at the next service station.

It was still sunny but very cold, and Matt sprinted from the van to the services to save his legs from getting too cold.

"Are you back at work tomorrow?" Matt asked.

"Yeah... It's pretty chilled at the moment though so it's okay. You're back working too, I guess?"

"Yeah, on delivery duty tomorrow".

We headed back to the van and sat down. Matt sighed at the remaining journey ahead of us.

"Okay. Another three hours and we're home. Good to go?" He asked.

I stared at his crotch, biting my lip.

"No...", he pointed his finger at me, but the accompanying cheeky grin on his face diminished any moral authority he was trying to convey. I massaged his left thigh across the van.

"We could nip in the back. We wouldn't lose that much time". I could see his hard on emerging through his shorts already.

Matt looked around. We had parked in a corner of a quiet service station. "Who says we need to nip in the back?"

I laughed. "It's broad daylight!"

"Nobody's here."

"Even for me that's bold".

Just as I contemplated it, a car drove towards us and parked nearby. We both laughed and wondered what might have been.

We nipped out of the van and ran around to the back doors. Matt opened them and followed me in. I quickly got on my knees and pulled his shorts down.

"I've been fucking dreaming of this for days". I said.

I moaned as his cock flung out of his shorts. He was dripping already. I took it deep in my mouth. My hand caressed his balls but he grabbed my hands and moved them further underneath towards his hole. I moaned and groaned at the unexpected surprise of being able to explore him more, and I could have shot a load myself in that brief moment.

I gently massaged his hole and dreamed of the moment when I might get to enjoy it even more.

Matt was clearly fucking horny too, and he wasn't hanging around. He started fucking my throat and grabbing my hair with his hands. He stopped for a second and gently pulled my head off his cock.

"I'm not being too rough am I?" He leant down to kiss me.

"Fuck my throat, you kind prick!" I replied.

He laughed and dragged my head back to his cock. Back and forth he rhythmically moved. I briefly wondered if his van was rocking back and forth and whether anyone outside had an inkling of what was happening inside.

"God I love your mouth mate".

Love. That was a new word for us, even in its partial use. It was an odd time to be wondering if I loved someone. Matt clearly had not thought anything of it. His eyes were shut as he pounded away. In a few moments time, he would be shooting down my throat and we would be back on the motorway home.

Yet I did love this. I did not immediately shut down the thought that was drifting around my mind: that perhaps I loved him.

Matt grabbed my hand and moved it back to his arsehole. I loved how demanding he was becoming, especially if he was demanding me to explore his hole.

I gently stroked his hole and gently held my finger just on the tip of his arse. In the absence of lube or my tongue, I didn't ease in any further.

Matt's pounding sped up as did his groans. He was grabbing my hair firmly now.

"Fuck. Mate. Don't stop. I'm gonna shoot. Oh fuck. Fu—. Fuck."

He shot a hot load right down my throat. A very wet load. That sort of load that is just too desperate and urgent to even think about being thick and creamy. It just needs to leave you. And now it was streaming down my throat.

Matt let go of my head but I wasn't quite done. I slowly sucked back and forth and took every last drop. I loved his cock so much.

That fucking love word again.

Matt was gently stroking my hair.

"Can I return the favour?" He asked.

"Later. Come on. Let's get home!"

We were both grinning as we left the back of the van and got back into the front.

We both kept smiling all the way home as we chatted about how hot that was and how he owed me one, and how he had enjoyed his hole being played with gently .

"You're becoming a good little gay, you know that?" I said.

He laughed. "Maybe I'm enjoying that".

Chapter Thirty Six

The drive south continued and even though it was mid-afternoon it was already starting to get dark as the cold, winter December nights drew in.

"So you told me in Glasgow that you were quite looking forward to calming things down a bit", I said.

"Yeah,". Matt replied.

"And now you've just spunked down my throat in the back of your van."

Matt burst out laughing.

"I mean... sure. But it's different with you. I'm calm doing anything with you".

I held his thigh as he said that. "Thank you. Me too".

"Tell me to fuck off if you want to but do you fancy hanging out tonight?"

"I would love that. Let's just chill out?" I asked.

"Yes, please", he replied.

We got back home and Matt parked up his van. We ran inside to avoid the cold, got up to my flat and I whacked the heating on. Matt ran to get a shower and I put the kettle on. We had a very lazy night of soup, sofa and TV. I even lit one or two candles for the occasion. Matt's head rested on my stomach while my fingers ran through his hair.

"You seemed to like my fingers around your arse earlier", I said.

"Yeah", he replied. "I've thought about doing that with you quite a lot lately. To be honest, I've thought for ages about different sensitive parts of my body that I have never really explored, but when there's nobody in your life at that moment that you trust, you just never explore it".

"I totally understand. I wasn't always the bottom bitch that's stroking your hair this evening you know, Matt?"

"Until your Mum showed me your baby photos, I just assumed you came out of the womb a slutty bottom".

Matt sat up and kissed me. He looked into my eyes and I looked into his. He kissed me again.

"I would love it if you played with my arse tonight".

"Yeah? Wait, is that why you were straight in the shower earlier?"

Matt laughed and nodded. "Maybe mate".

"You sexy fucker!" I grabbed his head and kissed him.

"I'm not promising anything though."

"I know. And nor should you. You can have thought about this for years but still not enjoy it. Or you do but it's just weird and we do more another time".

"Thank you".

"Now get your pants off."

Matt laughed and stood up. He dragged me off the sofa, turned the TV off and pulled me next door to my bedroom.

He took off his hoodie and his shorts. He stood naked in front of me. His cock was soft, which was very understandable as he'd shot gallons down my throat just a few hours earlier.

"You're such a beautiful man, you know that?" I said.

Matt smiled. He kissed me. I was so much more affectionate with him than I had been with anybody before. His hand ran down my cheek.

"How do you want me?"

"Lay down on the bed, face down".

"Arse up?"

"Slut. Not yet".

He laughed and lay down on the bed. I decided it would be nice to massage him. I took some oil and gently massaged his legs. Matt smiled and rested his head on my pillow. I oiled up his calves. His legs were stunning. They are so tight. If he was a footballer, I would just spend the whole ninety minutes looking at them, wondering what sights awaited you underneath the shorts and socks.

And here I was, fully aware of what else lay underneath his clothes as Matt submitted his body to me. His legs glistened with oil in the low lamp light of my bedroom. I massaged his left calf then his right. Then both together with my palms.

"This feels amazing mate", he said.

"Just don't fall asleep," I replied. "You'll get the fright of your life when I finger your arsehole".

He laughed and I could see him close his eyes. I worked my way up his legs so that my hands were now firmly massaging his thighs. I was absolutely not a trained massage therapist but I had done this quite a few times before. But not with somebody who I cared about so deeply.

I moved from his right thigh to his left. I spread his legs a little and enjoyed moving ever inward with my hands. I couldn't see his cock as he had placed it under his torso, but I could see his beautiful arse, balls and legs. Fuck, what a gorgeous man.

Although his legs were not very hairy, there were nice little tufts of hair around his arse. I loved it. I wiped his legs clean with a towel so that the massage oil would not get in the way too much, nevermind potentially damage a condom later on.

"You doing okay?" I asked.

"Yeah mate it's amazing," he sighed in reply.

I smiled. It is.

I put a little bit of lube on my fore finger and gently placed it on Matt's hole. Matt moaned. I just massaged it to get it wet. No insertion yet. I took the side of my hand and gently moved it up and down his arse crack. I believe some people call this the credit card swipe. Either way, it was clearly relaxing and riling Matt in equal measure.

I sat over his lower back, facing his arse. I rubbed his legs at the same time, my body falling down as my hands went from his glutes to his thighs to his calves, before coming back up in the opposite direction. I gently spanked his arse. Matt moaned.

I jumped back to sit on my knees between Matt's legs, just south of his arse. I kissed his left cheek. I kissed his right cheek. I kissed his lower back. I kissed his cheeks just above his hole.

I gently rested my tongue on his hole.

"Oh fuck!"

I suddenly remembered Queer As Folk again. "Nobody told you about that, did they?" I pondered in my mind, as I slowly worked my tongue up and down his hairy hole, each time resting just a little more deeply inside. Then a little more lube, a little more fingering, then back to my tongue.

I could rim Matt all night. If he ended up not taking my cock tonight, or any night, I did not care one bit. This view, this experience, this was amazing.

I got more primal in my rimming. My tongue mixed with my lips and stubble to give Matt's hole a range of textures. Matt was gripping the bed sheets and moaning more, and more and more.

I lubed up a finger and gently slid Matt's hole. He pushed me back but only slightly. I held firm, not pushing further but not giving way either.

"Just breathe", I said.

Gradually his arse got comfortable and I eased my finger and back and forth. He got comfortable. My left hand massaged his back while I gently finger fucked him.

"You doing okay?"

Matt nodded without really saying anything.

More lube. A second finger. More moans. My fingers were now firmly nestled in Matt's hole and he was taking it like a queen.

I flipped him over. Two fingers straight back in, he went to moan but I kissed him first to feel his moans fall deeply down my throat. I gently pounded his arse with my fingers while I kissed his neck, then again kissed his lips. In yet more 1990s cult TV and film references, I was reminded again of the hot finger fucking lesbian scene in Bound. That culminated in an orgasm. We were not there yet.

"Do you want to try it?" I asked.

His hand gently reached over to my cock. "Yes mate. Slowly."

I smiled. I lubed up his hole some more and put a condom on.

"I had assumed you would be on PrEP", Matt said.

"I am. We can discuss bareback in time but not tonight".

Matt smiled and nodded.

"Now, just relax and keep breathing. I will do it slowly and gently. If you feel unsure but not in pain then just breathe and trust me. But if it gets uncomfortable or painful, just tell me".

Matt nodded again.

I raised his legs a little.

"I'm staying on my back?" Matt asked.

"I want to look at you", I smiled in reply.

I looked down at his gorgeous body. His cock was hard and his body so inviting. I eased my cock in slowly, slowly, slowly. I rested the tip just inside his hole.

I could see, hear and feel Matt's breathing. I held my cock there to let his hole initially resist then gradually accept, then gently pushed in further as his hole relented. My lubey and vigorous finger fucking had helped. I lubed the back of my cock a little more until I was halfway in. He pushed me back a little but again, only a little.

He smiled. "It's okay. Keep going".

I eased in just a little further. I slowly fucked him back and forth, going no deeper than I had been. His arse took me a bit more straightforwardly than I might have hoped.

"I think you're finding this a bit too easy," I said.

"I don't know about that. Just gently".

Matt still breathed heavily and I could see that he was working hard to relax.

I sped up a little and went a little bit deeper. I was probably about four or five inches in at this point.

"You're doing great."

"Are you fully in?"

"I'm... about four sevenths!"

"Four sevenths?!"

We laughed. I took my opportunity as he was relaxed and laughing to ease in further all the way.

"Oh wow fuck," he moaned

"Make that five or six sevenths! You feeling okay?"

"Yeah. It's so weird. But nice. But uncomfortable".

"Yeah. That's about right for the first time".

I leaned over and kissed him. I leaned back and grabbed his thighs. I started to fuck him harder and his moans intensified.

I still wasn't all the way in, and I doubted I would be tonight. But it is a wonderful feeling when you see somebody relax and trust you, in a way that they have never trusted somebody before. Their smile and their energy, as they get rewarded for trusting you as they enjoy and savour the moment. That was mine and Matt's moment right now.

I started to pound him a bit more and he took it well. This was not easy for him but he was feeling new sensations that rose above any issues. He was also rock hard. I grabbed his cock. He brushed me away.

"No mate. Just focus on my arse for now".

It's hard to convey to you in writing how the moans and groans changed. But they gradually became more surprised, more aroused, more involuntary as I fucked him harder. He appeared to be enjoying becoming a bottom.

"I wanna sit on you", he said.

We quickly switched positions. I added more lube and he hopped straight on. Within a moment he was close to being cock deep, and suddenly realised that a new position meant a new angle and sensations - good and bad - that he was not fully ready for.

"Fuck. That's big!" He eased up a little, laughing.

"It's okay. Just build it up slowly".

He gently rode me until he got used to the new position. I took a second to savour the view in front of me. His hair, flopping back and forth. His face was focused on doing this well but also relaxing and grinning with pleasure. His body, glistening with sweat and dripping down his body to his cock, rock hard and dripping pre-cum. Then his legs, wrapped around my hands. I was a fucking lucky man.

"Hey Tom".

"Hey Matt".

He leaned down to kiss me but I was enjoying becoming a dominant top. I pounded him hard while his head was close to mine looking intently at me. His mouth opened as he realised I was fucking his arse hard and that he was taking it like a bitch. I loved it.

His moans got so loud that I was worried Mrs Barnstable might come up and complain. He never stopped staring deep into my eyes, except to briefly close them as he gasped for air.

"I love you, Tom".

He looked deeply into my eyes as he said it. It took me a moment to realise that he had said it at all, given how intensely engaged I was at the time.

I slowed down my fucking and looked deeply back at him.

Matt spoke to me again. "You absolutely do not need to say it back if you don't wa..."

"I love you too, Matt".

Matt smiled and there was silence as we just looked at each other. We were both motionless.

"Wow. Big moment", he said.

"Yeah," I smiled as I replied.

We kissed.

"What do we do now?" He asked.

I started to gently pound him again. "We do this, lover boy!".

Matt moaned, largely with pleasure but also with the hint of a man who was struggling to take my cock any further.

"I think we might need to stop now!" He smiled as he gently eased himself off me.

"You did well! How do you feel?"

"A bit like I might walk like John Wayne for a few days! But good".

Matt sat on my thighs and started to slowly wank his cock. I laid down and did the same. My cock was throbbing and I readied myself to shoot a big load, given how long it had been.

Matt beat me to it. "Fuck. Mate, I'm close".

I groaned and took my moment for us to come together. His load shot out - this one a little creamier and less urgent than the one a few hours earlier - just a moment before I shot too. Matt's facial expression went from pleasurable relief at his own eruption to laughter as he saw my own load fly out. The first gush hit my chin, the second the bedpost behind me, the third my neck and the rest all of my stomach. My body was convulsing in agonising pleasure, and Matt was very much amused as I struggled to contain my movements.

He smiled and chuckled as he reached for the tissue to clean me down. We showered and got back into our underwear and got straight into bed.

"Are you comfortable saying you love me?" He asked. "I won't be hurt if it was just said in the moment".

"I've wondered about it for a little while," I replied. "I don't say it with a host of expectations. But I feel it, and I like it. So yeah, I think I love you. Fucking deal with it".

"Ha! I love you too mate".

He kissed me on the forehead and we faced each other in bed, stroking each other and smiling.

Chapter Thirty Seven

Six months on.

Matt and I have just returned from Berlin, where we had a week away on holiday together. We went to pubs, went to a few clubs, and we saw a few sights. No threesomes, no swinging, no big sex parties. Just a relaxing time where any sexual encounters were in the privacy of our hotel room.

"Glad to be home?" I asked, as we got back home from the airport.

"Yeah. This has been great but I'll be glad to get back". Matt held my hand as he replied.

We are now a couple. It is all still very slow and very early days. Matt still lives with his brother, sister-in-law and niece. He is still figuring out what his job looks like after the pandemic. He still splits his time between delivery work and house moves. It will take time to adjust to what life and work looks like for him.

I still work predominantly from home, although I am forcing myself out into the office more and more. I am seeing friends again, I am putting structure back into my life.

And we are both working out what a relationship is. We haven't firmly decided whether our relationship is open or closed yet. It maybe does not need to be so firmly one or the other. On occasion, we may be horny and things may happen. For Matt's sake, he is taking it slow and trying to keep an open mind. For my sake, I am temporarily closing the door on random hookups, and together we will keep the conversation open.

Matt has met my parents again. They adore him, and he adores every single baby photo my mother shows him. I have yet to meet Matt's parents. That is a step for another day. I have met his friends though. They have made a real effort to get to know me, and they all seem to think Matt is happier than he has been in a while. I have seen Claire on one or two nights out. She understood, and we're okay.

We are also figuring out what our own sexual preferences are. Matt's hole has become gradually more relaxed, although he enjoys bringing out his dominant side. No matter how much I try and pretend I might be the dominant top of the pair, deep down I know I will be his bottom bitch whenever he wants me.

As we settled down after getting home from the airport, we both got ready to go back to work the next morning.

I occasionally reflected on what might have been: what if Matt had gone for a piss in Mrs Barnstable's flat instead of mine? What if I had flirted with him in our first encounter and he ran away?

But, this is how my story played out. And this - for now - is where it ends.

After weeks and months of distinguishing between love and lust, I am currently in love with a most wonderful man. I never have huge expectations of what will happen for me, Matt or anybody, but right now we are happy and having a gay old time.

At that moment, the doorbell rang, and I knew that nothing would match the moment when Matt came up the stairs and walked through my door.

I ignored it. Mrs Barnstable can answer it instead.

Reviews are so important to authors. They make more people aware of the book and they provide invaluable feedback to the author. If you can, please leave a review wherever you obtained a copy, or in the most appropriate channels. Thank you.

If you enjoyed this book, you may also enjoy other works by Arnold J. Miles. Visit www.lgbtqwriting.com[1] for more information about the author.

Text copyright: Arnold J. Miles, 2024.

Production copyright: Arnold J. Miles, 2024.

---

1. http://www.lgbtqwriting.com